George Hardy Tatam

The Buggy

Mr. Turnbull`s adventures in the new world

George Hardy Tatam

The Buggy
Mr. Turnbull`s adventures in the new world

ISBN/EAN: 9783744786102

Printed in Europe, USA, Canada, Australia, Japan

Cover: Foto ©Andreas Hilbeck / pixelio.de

More available books at **www.hansebooks.com**

"THE BUGGY;"

OR,

MR. TURNBULL'S ADVENTURES IN

THE NEW WORLD.

A SERIO·COMIC ROMANCE, IN RHYME.

BY

GEORGE HARDY TATAM.

LONDON:

MAIR & SON, 34, BEDFORD STREET, STRAND,

AND

22, HENRIETTA STREET, COVENT GARDEN, W.C.

1860.

CONTENTS.

"THE BUGGY:"

A Poem.

CANTO I.

I.

AFTER experience of my versic powers,
  I find I don't excel in the sublime—
My muse is comic, and profusely showers
  Her choicest gifts, when called on, any time—
True she can sing of love, and ladies' bowers,
  And when she does so, makes a pretty rhyme,
But still her *forte* is comedy. The serious
She shuns as something highly deleterious.

II.

And so here goes. At once upon the Sea
  Of Poesy my Fairy Vessel floats—
Her masts erect, her proud flag flying free—
  To skim thro' Helicon the best of boats
She'll prove herself ere long to all to be
  As this, my fancy's flight itself denotes—
An accident I sing, which once I met with
When in a Buggy I a friend was set with.

III.

Reader, if thou hast ever travell'd far,
  Perhaps thou'st seen Toronto's pleasant city—
'Tis by thy waves, Ontario, which are,
  When by the sunbeams kissed, to gaze on, pretty—
Nor does Toronto's Bay the landscape mar
  Nearly surrounded by a natural jetty,—
With just a narrow entrance to the port,
Of many a craft and steamer the resort.

B

IV.

Well! in my youthful days, I there was staying—
   'Tis good while young some travel to enjoy—
It much improves the mind; and is but paying
   The price for knowledge—which like maiden coy—
Requires much courtship—unto none displaying
   Its charms without he winning art employ,—
Instruction seeking, therefore, I left home,
A lad in years, in Western climes to roam.

V.

Ingenuous youth, from this our sea-girt isle,
   Make once, at least, a Continental tour—
I speak of those who, blest with Fortune's smile,
   Know not the meaning of the words—" I'm poor "—
Money their aid, a few months they beguile
   In viewing Europe from their carriage door,
Returning home so many travell'd zanies,
They prove how strange an animal a man is.

VI.

But I was poor—how else were I a poet?—
   'Tis odd that nature gave me the desire
To see far lands and nations strange, altho' it
   Costs much to those who travelling admire.
Such was my passion—nor could I forego it,—
   So scraping up what cash I might require,
I went to Canada instead of Italy,
And soon was where Toronto's thriving city lay.

VII.

I thought t'would cheaper be to travel where
   Infant society was not arrived
At that perfection when it is its care
   As much to pocket, as can be derived,
Of cash—from trav'llers having it to spare—
   By which means Europeans have contrived
Of stout John Bull to make a pretty penny
By of o'ercharges quite a miscellany.

VIII.

But to resume—I was then at Toronto
  Spending my leisure, eke a little money—
In search of recreation I had gone to
  Places whose Indian-sounding names would stun ye,
And after wand'ring a long time had grown to
  Require repose, and so in this good town I
Took up my quarters at the best Hotel,
Where I was fed and lodg'd extremely well.

IX.

And was assembled there a joyous knot
  Of youths, and old men, and of middle age
Some human specimens, with many a plot
  T' improve their state in life and earn them wage;
With some who, like myself, car'd not a jot
  In the pursuit of lucre to engage—
Some spent their days in pleasure, some in business—
Some sober were—some drank themselves to dizziness.

X.

T'was summer—summer there is past a joke—
  Not like our English imitation faint
Of summers—in whose Dog-days coat or cloak
  Is oft-times felt by no means a restraint:
But summer which with thirst nigh makes you choke,
  Parches your lips, and gives the meat a taint.
Not Paradise itself can give a nobler
Luxury then—than is a Sherry-Cobbler.

XI.

Oft when my thirsting lips have felt to be
  Like leathern fences to preserve my teeth—
When my furr'd tongue and mouth could scarce agree
  T' allow my lungs thro' them to draw a breath—
Oft have I deem'd that no felicity
  Either in Heav'n above or Earth beneath,
Could be compar'd to sucking thro' that straw,
By which the Cobbler to your lips you draw.

XII.

Oh! Yankee-land.   Oh! Yankee-land!   We smile
    At thy eccentric men and curious ways—
Thy customs would be laugh'd at in our isle;
    Nor would thy manners gain the meed of praise.
But one may travel weary mile on mile,
    May thirst and hunger many, many days
In England, till exhausted nature shrink,
Nor find thy sweet variety of drink.

XIII.

Thy Cobbler, Julep, and thy Cocktail are
    To thirsty souls perfection in their way;
And he may bless indeed his lucky star
    Who can refresh him with them every day—
When the sun scorches him, there is the bar
    Affording means of moistening his clay—
And if by Temperance he's rendered nice
He can have water there sublim'd with ice.

XIV.

Each clime affords to man a grand production—
    Holland its liquor, France its laughing wine,
These both are deem'd delicious in the suction—
    Both to their makers give ot wealth a mine;
Who, without them, would find a great reduction
    Of riches which do in their coffers shine.
America can also please the throttle
With drinks as glorious as Anti-teetotal.

XV.

And now, my muse, let us resume our story,
    Or men will think we bibulous have grown;
And that thy inspiration is a glory
    By taking stimulants upon me thrown;
And that my glass makes me thus dilatory
    In writing fairly out what should be shown,
Lest any such a false impression take,
Know, drinking water, I these verses make.

XVI.

A beauteous morning dawn'd upon the world,
The sun shone brightly and the sky was blue,
The wavy mists which on the lake were curl'd,
Melted in wreaths as the day onward drew.
Full many a bark, with canvas neatly furl'd,
Lay by the quay where loung'd their motley crew ;
The lake's clear waters, mirror of the sky,
Exposed their secrets to the gazer's eye.

XVII.

It was the Sabbath morn. No busy hum
Disturb'd the silence—the deserted streets
Confess'd the day of rest to man was come ;
That day the toil-worn lab'rer gladly greets,
For then rejoicing in his quiet home
His love-fraught glance his wife and children meets,
For on that day alone of all the week,
He may repose and recreation seek.

XVIII.

The tinkling bells, a jubilee to man,
From many a tow'r sonorously proclaimed ;
And now a crowd the observer's eye might scan,
On holy errand, nor of it asham'd,
As well-attir'd they their walk began
To church or chapel as his creed each fram'd.
The streets that lately were a solitude
Again receiv'd a thronging multitude.

XIX.

Which multitude all calmly walk'd and slow,
Save where a morning loit'rer hurried by,
Having at home remain'd till forc'd to go,
By warning bell, to raise his pray'r on high ;
Or where another, scorning outward show
Of Piety, prepar'd the town to fly,
And in the woods and by the streams to seek,
One day of rural pleasure in the week.

XX.

I issu'd forth and walked amidst the crowd,
 A stranger amongst strangers, from a land
Whose hardy sons may well indeed be proud
 To see their offspring on this distant strand,
With the same spirit as their sires endow'd,
 Raising their weekly pray'rs with impulse grand
To the Almighty in that nervous tongue,
Which e'er shall England's glorious name prolong.

XXI.

And this reminds me, a short time before
 An incident occurr'd which made my heart
Expand with pride and pleasure that thy shore,
 Albion, to me a birth-place did impart.
Those who cross seas and distant lands explore
 In some unheard of spot a subject start
For conversation, which to memory brings
Thoughts of past scenes to which she fondly clings.

XXII.

With some the feeling is regret for home—
 That home, which when 'twas near they viewed with scorn,
Now dimly seen across the ocean's foam—
 Themselves with wand'ring heart-sick and forlorn—
How like a strain of music does it come,
 By gentle zephyrs magically borne—
A melody—"The light of other days!"
Back to their hearts that brings—the past displays.

XXIII.

In some 'tis waken'd by a face—an eye—
 Or the description of some maiden fair,
Which draws from lover's heart the pent-up sigh,
 And makes him wish he had his lov'd one there—
Or rather, homeward-turning he drew nigh
 Her presence, who has sworn his fate to share—
For let them sneer who will, I say, that no man
Has tasted joy who has not lov'd a woman.

XXIV.

To those, whom from their fatherland have driv'n
Civil commotion or rebellion rude,
This feeling paints the fields where they have striv'n—
And many a pang will on their hearts intrude
Hopelessly exil'd—violently riv'n
To them are ties to be no more renew'd.
Oh! how delightful looms that cherish'd shore,
Which they are doom'd to visit—never more.

XXV.

Others again have left a wife behind,
And prattling children, who around their knees
Would press at evening, clamouring for a kind
Expression or fond look, like clustering bees.
Of this remembrance comes across their mind,
Which the sweet picture all-despairing sees,
For mountains rear their crests, wide oceans rage,
'Twixt them and thou who all their thoughts engage

XXVI.

To some this feeling is a gush of joy,
When from a stranger's lips good tidings flow—
A father hears the praises of his boy—
A son some friend of yesterday bestow
Praises upon his sire—without alloy
With pleasure, this, his bosom makes to glow.
His country's triumphs a brave warrior learns
By chance, and with his pristine ardour burns.

XXVII.

Such joyful feeling crept into my breast,
My country's praise in foreign lands to hear
Reverence for her by foreign lips exprest,
This well-nigh drew from eyes long dry a tear.
'Twas in the midst of wine and song and jest
The graceful tribute gratified my ear:
Graceful, for he who paid it kindred claimed
With a race conquer'd by the land he nam'd.

XXVIII.

We were a joyous company on board
  A steamboat up th' Ottawa briskly sailing;
Here Nature does her choicest charms afford,
  With loveliest scenery the traveller hailing;
Here wood and water and the land are stor'd
  With beauties it would take a month detailing—
Dense forests, frowning rocks, and waterfalls,
Where Solitude Primaeval man appals.

XXIX.

In many a pool and on the marshy sward,
  The Bull-frog's croaking fills the ear of might;
Far as he gazes round, by silence aw'd,
  Save for these sounds, and now and then the flight
Of birds whose throats did never yet afford
  A cadence, to the voyager no sight
Appears, but trees whose dense impervious shade
Is in a dark and death-like mass display'd.

XXX.

And so I glided as up Lethe's stream,
  But not to me was loss of memory giv'n;
Pacing the deck alone, my boyhood's dream
  Of future Glory and on Earth a Heav'n
Possess'd me. In my rapture nought did seem
  So high, t' attain it, it should not be striv'n—
Wealth, Power, and the smile from beauty's eye
Were surely mine as Fancy pictur'd by.

XXXI.

Oh! that those dreaming days could come again—
  With all their blest illusions! What delight,
Led by " imagination's airy train,"
  Then, as I walked, entranc'd my soul that night—
What years of cank'ring sorrow, care, and pain,
  Upon me since have cast their withering blight—
Yet memory clings with fondness to that hour
Ere yet misfortune's clouds began to lower.

XXXII.

The moon was shining in the beauteous sky—
A silver crescent in the blue profound—
The stars around their queen in groups did lie,
Twinkling and sparkling the horizon round—
The low night breeze "'rapt Nature's Lullaby"
Made, and the Paddle-wheels, the only sound.
All was so calm, so still, so death-like there,
From Earthly thoughts I turn'd, and breath'd a pray'r.

XXXIII.

A pray'r!—for surely, in that hour and place,
Thoughts of Omnipotence must intervene.
Below the sleeping earth—above, all space
Confess'd no *chance* had fram'd that goodly scene,
The Atheist there would feel compell'd to trace
Where the Eternal's hand at work had been.
Soften'd and charm'd, at length, I turn'd away
Into the cabin—to conclude the day.

XXXIV.

And so in social converse round we drew;
Each nam'd his native land and prais'd her sons—
The Scotchman eloquent on Scotland grew—
The Irishman o'er Erin's glories runs—
The Yankee boastful, almost ceas'd to chew,
While he proclaim'd America's "Great Guns"—
The Frenchman, fir'd with all a Gaul's vivacity,
Talk'd loudly of his nation's great capacity!

XXXV.

The Spaniard gave a recapitulation
Of all the glory which his sires had gain'd,
What time Columbus open'd to his nation
A world which long secluded had remain'd;
The Dutchman, smoking in his country's fashion,
Claim'd the proud place which Holland has attained-
By industry and skill in naval matters,
And commerce, which such wealth and plenty scatters.

XXXVI.

In short, each country a defender there,
    Found in some child or other of its soil—
England alone was left without a share
    Of praise, for I a long time did recoil
From taking any part in the affair,
    Dreading the evening's harmony to spoil—
Until, at length, a stranger from the west,
With much civility, me thus addrest :—

XXXVII.

"Sir, why thus silent are you while each man
    His country mentions and proclaims its praise?
I've waited since the argument began
    To know what nation honour'd was to 'raise'
So courteous, so complete a gentleman,
    With whom I've spent the pleasantest of days."
"Since then," replied I, "you thus me importune,
To be an Englishman I've the misfortune."

XXXVIII.

"Misfortune," cried the stranger who'd address'd me,
    "I'd give my worldly wealth and wander o'er
The earth in rags, nor care what clime possess'd me,
    Could I claim kindred with that glorious shore—
Of British feeling nothing can divest me,
    French was my sire—the mother that me bore
Was also French, but I am English quite—
I hate a Yankee—England's my delight.

XXXIX.

"I speak no French.   My days have ever been
    Spent among English in yon Western wild.
A Protestant—I'm every Sunday seen
    At church, and with me there my wife and child.
My wife is English also, and I mean
    My son a thoro' Briton shall be styl'd.
I wonder then to hear a Briton-born,
Speak of his father-land in terms of scorn."

XL.

" My friend," said I, " this company are all
　　Impressed with the idea that each is blest,
Because the lot on him has chanc'd to fall
　　To claim the country which he has confess'd—
My nation does not need, thank God! a brawl
　　To make the world believe it is the best.
I therefore spoke in irony; but you
Have given to England what I think her due.

XLI.

" Now in that country's name which you have prais'd
　　My thanks I give you from the inmost core
Of this my heart—delighted and amazed
　　To hear a stranger to my native shore—
One who on Albion's cliffs has never gaz'd,
　　Thus blessings on her and on her sons implore.
All comment I could make would now seem vanity,
After your speech conceiv'd with such urbanity."

XLII.

And upon this I crept into my berth,
　　Leaving the gay carousers o'er their glass,
Prouder than ever of that spot of Earth
　　Where I my boyhood and my youth did pass—
I slept but little, for the din of mirth
　　Rang in my ears all jocund as it was.
But in my memory I've treasur'd since
The noble heart that stranger did evince.

XLIII.

Well! I was going to church—but went astray—
　　Not *morally*, but *mentally* to tell
The story you have just been reading—pray,
　　Have I not told it excellently well ?
And now I will proceed upon my way
　　To church where me invites the organ's swell—
The congregation, at the door and in,
Are crowding to confess their weekly sin.

XLIV.

'Twas the cathedral church and dedicate
　To that Apostle who was hight St. James—
Kept in repair without the aid of rate
　Which England's Church in England so much shames—
But on its structure to expatiate
　Knowledge of building more than I have claims—
Suffice it to observe that it was spacious
And well adapted to the art loquacious.

XLV.

It chanc'd upon the day that I was there
　The Bishop of the diocese did preach—
I have forgotten just exactly where
　The text was which he took the truth to teach—
But I remember from the opening prayer
　To when had ceas'd the accents of his speech,
I thought a pulpit cushion ne'er put paw on
A better preacher than was Dr. Strachan.

XLVI.

The church was fill'd.　The audience were array'd
　In decent garments, and no doubt pertain'd
To that class which is call'd the " upper grade"
　Here, as in England ; and, of course, disdain'd
To mix with those who wield the axe and spade-
　So much of ancient custom is retain'd
In Trans-Atlantic regions as at home,
All thro' the colonies tho' you should roam.

XLVII.

And let me tell the artizan who dreams
　Of an equality beyond the sea,
Which to his cozen'd gaze delightful seems
　That no Republic, howsoever free,
With such abundance of good feeling teems
　As makes the affluent and the worker be
Equal—apart plac'd all respect to pelf—
Where a man loves his neighbour more than self.

XLVIII.

Let a man travel that Republic o'er,
　The grandest in expanse the world has seen,
From the Pacific to the Atlantic shore,
　From Maine to where upon the water's sheen
Of thy Gulf, Mexico, gleams many an oar;
　And when the toilsome journey he has been,
He will confess, if he have any candour,
Dollars alone are requisite for grandeur.

XLIX.

No Cincinattus, in those Western lands,
　Is call'd by Senates from behind the Plough :
There Washington himself a memory stands
　Alone in glory—no such men are now —
Dollars are solely grasp'd for by all hands—
　Golden's the laurel which adorns each brow,
And public Virtue would be scorned in rags,
If Vice produced his store of money-bags.

L.

For dreams Utopian nowhere can be found,
　For one not obstinate a better cure,
Than just America to travel round,
　And thus a knowledge of each state procure—
He'll find more freedom upon British ground
　Than where, with semblance false, Republics lure,
And become prouder of his native land
Each step he takes upon an alien strand.

LI.

Alas! my muse, my dilatory muse!
　Philosophising here you are again;
Your style is, past forgiveness, too diffuse,
　To tell your story you attempt in vain —
Just when your reader the main-thread renews,
　Off you are scamp'ring in a different strain.
Tell us your tale, but spare us your reflections,
To which might offer all sorts of objections.

LII.

And then my muse replies, as ladies will,
　　" I'll have my way—I'll do just as I please ;
My reader with Philosophy I'll fill,
　　And tell my tale at my own proper ease "—
What can I say then to her ?   I must still
　　Follow her promptings, and by slow degrees
The plan of my great argument unfold,
Embracing how—I from a Buggy roll'd.

LIII.

I left the church, and joining in the throng,
　　Along the street pursued my homeward way,
Fair dames and gallant gentlemen among,
　　Who as they walk'd indulg'd in converse gay—
The distance to my hostelrie was long,
　　But not unpleasant on so bright a day ;
The air was warm, but yet not overpowering,
So that I had an appetite devouring.

LIV.

Hunger! the rich man courts thee as a boon,
　　The poor man thee esteems his direst foe ;
Whose infant mouth is fill'd with silver spoon,
　　Will never p'rhaps thy dreadful cravings know—
While Poverty's gaunt child can, scarce a noon,
　　Procure a dinner, but must empty go—
Pleasure thou art to one, to t'other pain,
So much from *circumstance* we lose and gain.

LV.

I have felt hunger—also appetite—
　　Hunger—until my fainting limbs refus'd
T' obey their owner, when my failing sight
　　Could with no certainty by me be us'd—
The stalest crust I grasp'd at with delight,
　　Nor of its stone-like hardness it accus'd—
At which mere appetite would turn its nose up,
Nor it allow its pamper'd mouth to close up.

LVI

And when I reach'd mine inn—a table spread
  With every dainty which that land affords,
Around a most enticing odour shed
  Of fish great plenty, and of wild-fowl hoards,
Mutton, and beef, and soup, and to be fed
  The guests the whole were eager making tow'rds—
Of vegetables too were beans and peas,
Besides potatoes quite as good as these.

LVII.

Those who have seen a Trans-Atlantic dinner,
  Such as is given at the best Hotels,
Will well know that the earliest beginner
  Feeds far more daintily than he who dwells
On ceremony and regards the sinner
  Sitting beside him; and the waiter tells
To fill his neighbour's plate before his own—
Such court'sy in America's unknown.

LVIII.

Your thoro' Yankee—(such indeed were there)
  With fell determination at the table
Himself ensconces—food his only care,
  And fills his belly fast as he is able—
To give his fellow-traveller a share
  Of what receives his maw insatiable,
Is not his business—Have not all their hands?
Before them equally the dinner stands.

LIX.

From this vile custom are the Yankee's styl'd
  Ee'n by their countrymen of better breeding—
"Bolters," from the precipitation wild
  Which they evince, whilst they're engag'd in feeding—
Nor to good manners are they reconciled
  At meals—because they're to Dispatch impeding—
Your Yankee wastes no time in mastication,
Eating with him's a swallowing operation.

LX.

At first when placed at table with a set
    Such as I mention, I felt "passing strange,"
I thought the men were eating for a bet,
    Hazarding their digestion to derange—
And that the ill by dollars would be met,
    And so their health they would for cash exchange,
But soon I found it was their daily custom,
And wondered much their dinners never burst 'em.

LXI.

But, by the time I speak of, I had grown
    Us'd to their ways, and acted on that use—
Thus to the table when I sat me down,
    Round me I look'd, determined not to lose
An instant my desires in making known
    So that attention prompt I might induce.
I got my plate fill'd, and with knife and fork
At once I fell right manfully to work.

LXII.

I need not say of what I there partook—
    What dish I favor'd, what untouch'd I left—
That which I ate did credit to the cook
    And from the board of half its bulk bereft
Was when removed—nor how " by hook or crook "
    My share of food I kept from neighbour's theft,
And manag'd a fair dinner to obtain,
Which some I notic'd struggl'd for in vain.

LXIII.

Suffice it, dinner ended, as must end
    This Canto of my Poem; for I find,
As I proceed such recollections blend
    With what to tell you I, at firs', design'd
That tho' for brevity I much contend
    And to diffuseness am nowise inclin'd,
My muse my mistress is, and leads me on
To write more fully than I should have done.

LXIV.

Therefore, my gentle reader, for a time
 I must to you say that " wild word " Adieu !
That which I've written I believe 's sublime,
 And, what is better, altogether true :
Another stanza, and my pleasing rhyme
 You'll have as I it from my fancy drew :
At least the opening Canto is completed,
To it your kind attention is entreated.

LXV.

Farewell!   The best of friends, we know, must part,
 But that from parting ne'er removes the sting,
Tho' the necessity wrings many a heart,
 Yet hopes of future meetings comfort bring
My reader (fair as gentle p'rhaps thou art !)
 I promise thee I have not ceas'd to sing ;
But soon another Canto shall delight thee,
Which I intend immediately to write thee.

END OF CANTO I.

C

CANTO II.

—

I.

THERE was a youth whom no poetic dreams
 Had e'er disquieted—a humdrum soul—
On whom the green woods and the murm'ring streams
 With nought of magical allurement stole—
And Nature which, to me enchanting seems,
 Could never him from plodding ways cajole.
His genius was anti-sentimental—
Our being friends a thing quite accidental.

II.

And yet I lov'd him; and he clung to me—
 We met at the Hotel where I was staying;
In nothing earthly did our thoughts agree
 Save in a mutual sympathy displaying.
He stuck to business—I, from business free
 In search of pleasure was all idly straying;
Yet in his hours of freedom he and I
Were ever to be found in company.

III.

There are who preach of sympathetic souls,
 And friendships firm by kindred spirits form'd:
Upon *their* theory fishes swim in shoals,
 And bees Platonic, by a sound, are swarm'd;
From love of grubbing miners dig for coals,
 Their hearts, of course, all fire-damp proof being warm'd;
The Blacksmith loves his fellow, and the Sweep
Will at a brother "sooty's" sorrows weep.

IV.

My own opinion differs much from theirs—
　How else were Duncan and myself such friends?
Men do not, I am sure, arrange in pairs
　Themselves, because an innate feeling bends
One tow'rds the other.—P'rhaps in some affairs
　Interest a common object to them lends;
But this creates no friendships—oft makes foes,
As ev'ry worldly man's experience shows.

V.

Far oft'ner minds the most contrasted meet,
　In friendship's ties to be no more dissolv'd.
Variety to every man is sweet.
　He who in worldly cares is much involved
Will, joyful, one who knows not of them, greet,
　To throw his mental burden off, resolv'd.
The cunning man respects his simple neighbour,
And his affection to obtain will labour.

VI.

I think, then, both in friendship and in love,
　The less similitude there is the better,
Consult your mirror, and my axiom prove—
　To your own face your eyesight would you fetter?
One tires of looking at the skies above;
　And even Venus, if you often met her,
Would seem less beautiful than when at first
She on your raptur'd eye celestial burst.

VII.

This is the reason, I presume, why ladies
　Withdraw themselves so oft from lovers' ken;
After the indelible impression made is,
　They flit before you and are gone again.
A woman to display herself afraid is,
　Too often to the earnest gaze of men,
For fear her loveliness should not bear scrutiny,
And her admirers thus, perchance, should mutiny.

VIII.

But let Philosophers the question settle
  By theorizing on it to their fill,
Facts are so stubborn, that o'er them they'll get ill,
  If to them they oppose their fancies still—
I know it stings your dreamer like a nettle,
  When demonstration contradicts his will ;
But my philosophy is quite Baconian,
I've no more speculation than an onion,

IX.

On this I pride myself, because I see
  The world around me as it really is—
I love it, though its ways may evil be,
  Misanthrophy on me confers no bliss,
The world's smile I ne'er court, nor ever flee
  From its derision as a serpent's hiss—
If it should giggle, I can join in laughter,
And if it mourn, I'm none the worse thereafter.

X.

This is your true Philosophy—all else
  Is idle dreaming, and disturbs repose,
A man deserves most richly cap and bells
  Who's always brooding o'er a hoard of woes,
With such as he are peopled madmen's cells,
  For this to madness by indulgence grows ;
I thank my stars my views of life are jolly,
Nothing's more farcical than melancholy !

XI.

Bill Duncan and myself, I said, were friends—
  'Tis for this reason that I call him "Bill"—
Familiarity, I know, offends
  Whose heads are stupid, and whose hearts are chill—
With such t' annihilate esteem it tends ;
  They speak as if they'd undergone a drill,
I love full liberty of conversation,
And all restraint's my utter detestation.

XII.

" Bill," I addressed him, as we rose from table
    (We'd been at dinner, you'll p'rhaps bear iu mind),
" A horse, you tell me, you have in the stable ;
    To take a journey I feel much inclin'd.
To get the landlord's Buggy we'll be able,
    And some spot worth a visit soon can find."
" Let not a doubt of that your thoughts cucumber,"
Was his reply ; " we'll drive out to the Humber."

XIII.

" Agreed," I said ; " I know the place you mention
    Is worth beholding ; let us then prepare."
He answered : " It shall be so—apprehension
    I have not any, if we promise care,
The landlord will oppose this our intention,
    But lend his Buggy, should we speak him fair ;
You change your dress—I'll go below and see him,
And if words will not gain our wish, I'll fee him."

XIV.

We separated. To my room I went,
    While Bill the landlord sought within the bar ;
Not many minutes at my glass I spent,
    And whilst engag'd there, left the door ajar,
Smiling at which my friend, on journey bent,
    Appear'd, his face effulgent as a star—
" The Buggy's borrow'd !" was his exclamation ;
" So now let's forward to our destination.

XV.

" The hostler in the yard is making ready—
    My driving coat's upstairs—I'll just go don it—
The animal I own is wondrous steady,
    And would obey a lady in a bonnet.
He goes with the precision of an eddy,
    Nor makes a fuss about it, having done it—
So that all thought of danger's out of question,
Let no alarm, then, injure your digestion."

XVI.

" Bill," my rejoinder was, " I am not nervous,
    And in equestrian exercise am skill'd ;
Your horse I have no doubt will nobly serve us,
    Being with good provender so amply fill'd."
This afternoon the people shall observe us
    (If but the Buggy be of decent build),
As to the Humber we so stylish dash on,
Our whole turn-out the very pink of fashion.

XVII.

" Be quick,—I'll take a pipe while you are dressing—
    You see how all-Adonis-like I stand ;
No Venus, I am sad to say, possessing—
    To love to wile me with caresses bland—
I need not waste our moments in confessing
    The Goddess should not me with coldness brand."
Quoth Bill, " I'm wholly of your way of thinking,
When Love's propitious I detest all shrinking."

XVIII.

He left me then, and I the stairs descended
    With rapid strides, nor look'd where I was going—
My headlong course, however, soon was ended,
    Its impetus a lady overthrowing.
Full twenty steps—our forms together blended—
    Downward we roll'd, nor knew what we were doing—
Love's dart in both our hearts at once did rankle,
We lost our hearts—and Harriet sprain'd her ankle.

XIX.

I was the first to rise. Before me lay—
    Her dress disordered by her sudden fall—
As sweet a girl as ever saw the day
    Trembling and faint. Her pallor did appal
My heart as her to aid I did essay,
    Giving assistance thro' that spacious hall :
My arm was thrown around her—her's embraced me,
In what a Paradise that tumble plac'd me.

XX.

We reach'd a room at last, and her fair form
    Upon a couch all tenderly I laid.
Her perfum'd breath my brow with moisture warm,
    Slightly suffus'd. Her pouting lips display'd
Within their coral her teeth's ivory charm—
    Her eyes as yet were hidden by the shade
Of their long silken lashes—while a tear
Did, like a pearl, upon their edge appear.

XXI.

She had not fainted—but I thought her fainting—
    I ran for water and a smelling bottle,
The female servants of our fall acquainting,
    Who, soon things requisite for ladies brought all,
When they're o'ercome. The scene was past all painting,
    One scream'd—I thought she would have split her throttle—
Another shouted " murder," and a third
All things improper with loud voice inferr'd.

XXII.

I kept them off as well as I was able,
    And sprinkled on her brow some drops of water.
The " Sal Volatile " I from the table
    Next took, which to her senses quickly brought her—
Her sweet eyes sent a glance inexplicable
    Thro' their moist lashes—when her mother sought her.
'Tis strange old ladies should drop in upon us
Just at the moment when we'd have them shun us.

XXIII.

But so it is, and this is fate's perversity,
    Which never can let lover's have their way—
But them accords a due share of adversity,
    That makes them fonder grow at each delay—
Meetings are sweeter from their very scarcity,
    When those who would prevent them are away.
A loving word—a kiss—a sigh or two,
Alas! what mischief such proceedings do.

XXIV.

When Harriet's mother came upon the scene,
    Her I accosted, ignorant of her name.
I fancied somewhere I her face had seen,
    But did not call to mind from whence she came.
As she approached, in haste, with angry mien,—
    While I look'd foolish, overpower'd with shame—
But Harriet from my awkwardness retriev'd me,
And as a friend her mother soon receiv'd me.

XXV.

I found I had a note of introduction
    From England to this very lady brought,
Which when produc'd—a different construction
    To place on our adventure she was taught—
To have my charmer mov'd she gave instruction,
    Who, leaning on me, her apartment sought—
Now this, *in lore,* was literally *falling*
Meanwhile Bill Duncan me aloud was calling.

XXVI.

Thro' the clos'd door I told him "I was coming"—
    The lady on a couch I had deposited.
Her pretty ankle her mamma was thumbing ;
    And, so engag'd, I quitted them, there closeted—
It was high-time, for on the panel drumming
    Was Bill—I op'd the door and found him close at it—
"The Buggy's all prepared—the horse is prancing,"
He said   be quick—the afternoon's advancing."

XXVII.

I left the room with Bill, and down the stairs
    Proceeded quickly, and the Buggy gain'd,
All inattentive to his urgent pray'rs
    That what had pass'd should be by me explain'd.
Disgusted with the aspect of affairs
    He mounted to the seat I had attained—
Ourselves we settled—Bill assum'd his whip
And reins—and then we started on our trip.

XXVIII.

Over the stones we rattled at a pace
Which us precluded from all conversation.
I thought of nothing but my charmer's face,
And Bill desired to reach our destination.
In silence thus we journey'd for a space,
Not e'en indulging in an exclamation ;
But when at last we'd issued from the city,
Bill thus address'd me in a tone of pity : –

XXIX.

" Poor fellow ! it is desperate I find,
This sudden passion for that tumbling lady ;
I half suspected something of the kind
As you detained me long when I was ready.
At first I thought of leaving you behind
To reap the harvest of your steps unsteady,
But afterwards I felt it would relieve you
This jaunt with me. Come, do not let it grieve you.

XXX.

" And now just tell me—what may she resemble ?
That horrid door prevented me from seeing ;
Of course all beauties in her face assemble,
As is the case with each angelic being :
I just observ'd her little white hand tremble
When from your farewell grasp you it were freeing.
Is all the rest as lovely as those fingers,
Whose perfect moulding in my memory lingers ?

XXXI.

" But have you learnt her birth and expectations ?
For these are truly most essential things ;
You are a gentleman and your relations——"
A squirrel here took flight on leathern wings,
Which made our steed exhibit some saltations
That shook the Buggy, and deranged the springs :
Bill to repair the damage made exertion,
And I assisted—glad of the diversion.

XXXII.

We found our horse's sudden freak had snatch'd
    A screw from its position—which being lost,
Could not, of course, as we were plac'd, be match'd.
    Thus our vehicle awry was toss'd,
And almost from one axle was detached,
    Which made us fear the chidings of our host;
The perspiration from our brows did trickle
With working—wern't we in a pretty pickle?

XXXIII.

Bill pull'd his hat off; and his steaming brow
    Wip'd with his handkerchief, and look'd around,
"What must we do to right us, Turnbull, now?"
    He said, while I sat panting on the ground.
I answer'd, "I'm as ignorant as a cow
    Of any remedy that can be found;
Had we a piece of rope we might secure it,
But we have not, nor know where to procure it."

XXXIV.

Just then a spiral wreath of smoke we spied,
    Above the foliage of the forest stealing.
"That rises from a hut," with joy, I cried;
    "And we can get a cord by there appealing."
"The plan's not bad," said Bill, "and must be tried,
    For we are in a ' fix,' there's no concealing
Here I'll remain, while you your luck try yonder
Observe your way, be sure, and do not wander."

XXXV.

I left Bill all disconsolately there,
    The fractur'd Buggy for his contemplation,
And knowing we had little time to spare,
    Of speed began to make great demonstration
I climb'd a snake fence, managing to tear
    In doing so, my left "continuation,"
And cross'd some clearings, soon the forest gain'd,
Then paused, and for the smoke my eyesight strain'd.

XXXVI.

Those who of forests have conceived a notion
    From the small plots of woodland England grows,
Will not behold, without intense emotion,
    Those trackless solitudes where Nature shews
Her centuries of verdure—like the ocean
    Vast—but more awe-inspiring in repose ;
Where daylight scarcely penetrates the density
Of the dark foilage, in that green immensity.

XXXVII.

'Tis true the forest I had wander'd o'er
    Far in the West ; but then 'twas with a guide—
Alone its various pathways to explore,
    Ere this adventure I had never tried.
Some small experience I had had before,
    And on its aid reluctantly relied ;
I followed the first opening which appear'd
The smoke to lead to, and by it I steer'd.

XXXVIII.

But soon 'twas lost to view, and then the place
    I thought it occupied the trees above,
Blue as the sky around, without a trace
    Of smoke my erring vision did reprove—
Quickly my eye swept the ætherial space,
    Hoping the smallest whiff might upward move
Alas ! 'twas gone ! a vapour had beguil'd me—
To turn about I almost reconcil'd me.

XXXIX.

When thus I reason'd. " Bill will be excited
    And I shall seem an object of derision
If I allow myself to be affrighted
    By the first obstacle." 'Twas my decision,
E'en tho' in searching I should be benighted
    To find the hut where smoke had struck my vision ;
With this intention I my path pursued
Amid the intricacies of the wood.

XL.

Some time I struggled on where'er there seem'd
A wider space between the trunks of trees,
On which the sunshine glancing downward stream'd,
And where my warm cheek met the gentle breeze.
The wild vines here and there festooning stream'd,
And the long rank grass clung around my knees ;
But still 'twas forest all, no op'ning beckon'd
To lead me to the hut on which I reckon'd.

XLI.

How long I wander'd thus I cannot say,
My limbs had weary grown, my brow perspir'd,
When just, as with the roughness of the way,
And its apparent endlessness I tir'd,
On my right hand there was a clearing lay,
Which *might* contain the hut that I desir'd ;
Thither I turn'd, and after some delays,
My footsteps led me to a field of maize.

XLII.

A stump I mounted, round I cast a look,
The clearing was extensive, and inclin'd
With gradual sweep, to a meand'ring brook
On whose green bank, just at a curve, enshrin'd,
All picturesquely, in a forest nook,
A farm-house stood—a model of its kind—
Its roof was shingled, and its walls were boarded,
And the farm-buildings with the house accorded.

XLIII.

" Now I'm all right," said I, and cheerful grew,
As walking round the maize I hastened on,
I clear'd a log-fence and my gladden'd view
Pastures exempt from timber broke upon
Unsightly stumps, at intervals 'tis true,
Displayed their blackness in the glaring sun,
And yet those jagged stumps, that wither'd sward,
Did to my vision great relief afford.

XLIV.

The eye grows weary with too much of shade,
    And welcomes a contrasted glare of light;
At first 'tis dazzled—but, accustom'd made,
    Hail's its effulgence with intense delight.
In pictures, when a sameness is display'd,
    Monotony of hue palls on the sight,
A landscape for this reason, needs variety.
Objects repeated oft beget satiety.

XLV.

'Twas easy walking to the streamlet's brink,
    The exercise, in fact, restor'd my vigour.
Its waters clear invited me to drink,
    And I, to moisten my parch'd lips was eager—
My pocket flask I in the wave did sink,
    And prov'd myself a most accomplished swigger—
That draught convinced me how replete with bliss
" A cup of water in the desert" is.

XLVI.

Refreshed, I leap'd the stream, and onward went,
    Up the ascent gaining the last enclosure—
A garden was before me—its extent
    Was limited, and southern its exposure—
The gate I open'd, and my footsteps bent
    To the house door, beneath a porch of osier,
Clinging round which were monthly roses blooming,
And with their scent the atmosphere perfuming.

XLVII.

I'd only time for casual observation,
    And noted but what met my hurried glance—
The premises seemed an approximation
    To English comfort—an unusual chance,
At that remote verge of civilization,
    And of all round them so much in advance.
The door I knocked at—to it quickly came
A stout old gentleman a little lame.

XLVIII.

To him in piteous accents I related
    The dire mischance which broke our Buggy's spring,
How my companion on the highway waited
    Till I rejoined him with some rope or string.
Thus our position having fairly stated,
    I asked him "could he give me such a thing?"
His answer was "Walk in, Sir, till I get it,
Just taste my whiskey, and you'll not regret it."

XLIX.

"You snam *fatuygued*" (he us'd a brogue Hibernian),
    We went into a room; and from the closet
He reach'd a flask of Ireland's Falernian,
    And pour'd into a tumbler a deposit.
"This is the liquor," he exclaim'd, "to journey on,"
    As with much gusto, *neat*, he down did toss it;
"Fill up your glass and then the rope I'll fetch you,
Meanwhile upon the sofa you may stretch you."

L.

I took some whiskey, which I drank diluted,
    And on the sofa stretch'd my weary frame—
My host then left me, and I felt recruited.
    Quick, with the rope I ask'd for, back he came—
He wish'd me, had it my convenience suited,
    To spend the day with him, and gave his name—
My name I gave too, my inviter telling,
At Stone's Hotel, Toronto, I was dwelling.

LI.

I ask'd him then to point a nearer way
    By which the spot I left I might attain,
Regretted time forbade my longer stay,
    And promis'd soon to visit him again.
A path he shew'd me where I could not stray,
    And where no forest could my steps detain.
I follow'd it with ease across the clearing,
Gaining the high-road on its edge appearing.

LII.

The road was bent into a gentle curve
 Just where our accident had taken place;
And when I left Bill, I contriv'd to swerve
 Into the forest not a little space.
This, in returning, I could well observe,
 And all the circle I had made could trace—
Once on the road, I onward press'd, proceeding
To where I found Bill,—and his hackney feeding.

LIII.

" What cheer ?"—he shouted loud, while at a distance,
 Puffing along the dusty way I toil'd—
" Have you procur'd the desired assistance ?"
 The rope I shew'd him on my shoulder coil'd—
He said, " our steed's enjoying his existence,
 While with this scorching sun I'm nearly broil'd.
If he had known the consequence of shying
In frolics he'd have been more self-denying."

LIV.

" Perhaps so," I replied, " a sage reflection !
 But one that wont our broken spring repair.
We'll set to work if you have no objection—
 I'll bind the fracture while you hold it there."
" Agreed," he answer'd, following my direction,
 And of the operation took his share—
The Buggy, by our efforts thus united,
Upon its axle soon again was righted.

LV.

When we had finished, we the work survey'd
 With sentiments of intense approbation—
" What ingenuity is here display'd !"
 Said Bill, regarding it with admiration.
His steed he then caught which, the while, had stray'd,
 Regardless of the toil his calcitration
Had brought upon us—'twixt the shafts he plac'd him,
And to the vehicle securely trac'd him.

LVI.

" Now," cried I, " had we better not return ?
    Observe the sun sinks see the day is waning—
And to a future time our trip adjourn;
    Do you intend abroad all night remaining ?"
But the idea with anger Bill did spurn,
    Saying, the Humber he was bent on gaining—
And hinting 'twas a wish to see my lady
That to go back again made me so ready.

LVII.

" Well!" I replied, " Bill, onward let us gaily,
    Not one am I to balk you of your whim—
With you I'll go wherever does the way lie,
    Only be cheerful, and don't look so grim—
As for my charmer, I can see her daily,
    Should I return, uninjur'd life and limb,
So mind your hackney.—See his ears he's pricking!
Or, in a ditch we soon shall both be sticking."

LVIII.

Quoth Bill, " I will "—and he applied the lash
    Most vigorously to his horse's flank,
Drawing his reins tight, as with sidelong dash
    We graz'd with one wheel a projecting bank—
Then, swifter than the summer-lightning's flash
    We cro-s'd the road and in a hollow sank.
Said I, " your driving needs of way much latitude,
And is remarkable for change of attitude.

LIX.

" But don't you think, going straight in one direction
    Will sooner bring us to our journey's end,
Than thus of circles wildly many a section
    Describing, which to nothing good can tend ?"
" I do," was his reply—" and now subjection
    Shall make my steed his mode of progress mend—
At length I feel his mouth—the pace is killing—
The old saw teaches " use the horse that's willing."

LX.

The road was level—in a line extending,
    A bank on one side and a stream on t'other
It from the forest on each hand defending—
    And now we pass'd a clearing—now another—
Now up a gentle rise the ground was bending—
    Now sinking where the dust us did nigh smother—
Th' excitement of the rapid locomotion
Induc'd in us of pleasure an emotion.

LXI.

Sage Dr. Johnson in high terms extoll'd,
    As one of life's chief pleasures—of a chaise,
While in the corner he securely loll'd—
    By two good roadsters on old England's ways
From stage to stage, when trav'ling to be roll'd,
    With nought to do but on the scene to gaze
And muse upon it, as it met his vision—
I think with him that feeling is Elysian.

LXII.

But still more glorious is the like sensation
    Beneath the bright sky of yon western land—
Your spirit feels a joyous elevation
    As thro' the woods you make your progress grand—
A Buggy, too, is of " Superior station"
    To an old " yellow-boy" bought, " Second hand"—
The roads are quite as good in many places
As those o'er which an English bagman races.

LXIII.

The landscape I'm describing has a sameness
    Because 'tis woodland all ; and yet a break
Of the dense foliage it relieves from tameness,
    Shewing the dark blue waters of the lake
When the sun plays upon them. But a lameness,
    Has seized my Pegasus—so you must take
Half a description of a lovely whole,
Could I, I'd finish it—upon my soul !

D

LXIV.

But after all! perhaps the faint outline
 I've limn'd so feebly, gives a better notion
Of that which I'm desirous to define ;
 And for the grand inspires more devotion—
Than if I'd tir'd you with attempts to shine—
 Who can describe the waters of the ocean ?
And who, in verse to the untravell'd eye,
Can aught like Forest Scenery supply ?

LXV.

The Sun had sunk, and on the topmost boughs
 Of the huge trees the moon was looking down ;
From the clear'd pastures homeward drove the cows,
 The sturdy hind to the adjacent town ;
When from my reverie I did arouse
 Myself, attracted by a milkmaid's gown,
Which with her hand she held as forth she stray'd,
And her neat ankle to our view display'd.

LXVI.

First a log hut or two amongst the trees
 Mingled their pale smoke with the evening haze ;
Then, indications of more worldly ease,
 Houses of framework did their gables raise :
And barns and cow-sheds in the rear of these,
 Built with great neatness met the stranger's gaze.
Stores touched the street, and taverns there invited us,
Which with the hope of food and rest delighted us.

LXVII.

The Humber dashing o'er a rocky bed,
 Frolics and sparkles in the moonbeam's play.
A small cascade, by tiny streamlets, fed
 Its tribute pours of water and of spray
Into the river, forming a mill-head,
 Thus useful made to man when on its way—
Below the mill stands—picturesque its site—
An object of much beauty by moonlight.

LXVIII.

We cross'd the river by a bridge of plank,
　　And pull'd up at a tavern we descried
Just to the left, upon the river's bank,
　　Where Bill assured me we should be supplied
With good refreshment ;—and the host would thank
　　Us for our custom did we there abide—
The ostler took our steed, as we alighted
In haste, for we had fear of being benighted.

LXIX.

The bar we entered—There we found mine host,
　　Of whom we made immediate demand,
If he could give us either boil'd or roast,
　　For to assauge our appetite we'd plann'd.
He said, of viand's cook'd he could not boast,
　　But a beefsteak before us soon should stand.
Each took a biscuit and a glass of sherry,　　·
Which I declared was good, and Bill said " very."

LXX.

We then were usher'd into a neat room—
　　The furniture was plain, but bright and clean ;
And the floor tokens shew'd of mop and broom,
　　As if it scour'd recently had been ;
Flowers and shrubs did in the window bloom,
　　And black as jet the polish'd stove was seen—
Upon the walls there hung a singing bird,
A likeness also of King George the Third.

LXXI.

As if to show too that our host was neuter
　　In politics, just opposite the King
We noticed him to monarchs ne'er a suitor,
　　But first the Crown's allegiance off to fling—
George Washington, for Princes a meet Tutor,
　　In a gilt frame was hung up by a string—
Thus after death *his portrait* was *suspended*,
A change of Fortune *him* might *so* have ended.

LXXII.

We sat us down to wait for our repast
   (A tidy servant-maid had brought us lights),
When Bill, the time to fill up of our fast,
   Began to tell me of the pleasing sights
The country round afforded—" When, avast ! "
   Cried I ; " What's that my sense of hearing smites ?"
I listened for the sound—which soon again
Fell on my ear—the clock was striking *ten*.

LXXIII.

" I'll tell you what," said Bill, " the hour is late—
   We'll take a bed here, and to-morrow go
To see a friend of mine, on an estate
   Not far from this, who'll us the country show ;
And, as you take an int'rest in my fate,
   And feel yourself th' effects of Cupid's bow,
I don't mind telling you I love his daughter,
Will you assist in my attempt to court her ?

LXXIV.

" I know you'll say that I have lur'd you here,
   With the intention I have just express'd,
But I declare, however, you may jeer,
   That no such thought at starting fill'd my breast—
But see, the landlord's bringing in our cheer,
   Give your consent, and set my mind at rest—
Toronto we shall reach to-morrow night,
Where I in my turn will your aid requite.

LXXV.

" Besides, there is a blacksmith's close at hand,
   Who in the morning will our spring repair—
The landlord here will let him understand
   We're gentlemen to whom the morning air
Is pleasant ; and with cash at our command,
   Which in the laudable desire to share,
He'll set to work with morning's earliest beam,
And do our job before we've ceas'd to dream."

LXXVI.

I never could deny a friend assistance—
    An easiness of temper is my failing,
And so to Bill's proposal small resistance
    I made—because I thought it unavailing—
And when before me was a steak, the distance
    Seem'd far to travel, after it assailing—
The first cut into it found me relenting,
The second *nearly*—the third *quite* consenting.

LXXVII.

Our supper soon we finish'd. To the stable
    Our way we wended there to view our steed,
Who munch'd his oats as fast as he was able
    As if to our resolve he quite agreed;
The moon shone brightly when we turn'd the gable,
    So downwards by the stream we did proceed
To see the rapid waters dashing, sparkling—
Now in our view—now flowing onwards—darkling.

LXXVIII.

How sweet it is at such an hour to stroll
    Alone with her who fills your ev'ry thought,
While on your ear the murm'ring waters roll,
    And by your eye their silvery play is caught—
Your arm around her—mingled soul with soul—
    The heart with sweet emotions is so fraught,
One can imagine seraphs from the skies
Stealing away to bask in woman's eyes.

LXXIX.

I thought this—but I dare not give expression
    To such reflections, fearing Bill would smile,
For I to him had never made confession
    I, poetising, did some hours beguile;
Such an amusement had been a transgression
    To him, and altogether puerile:
So silent I remain'd and even Duncan
Into a moody reverie was sunken.

LXXX.

And then we paus'd, and gaz'd upon the stream,
  The woods, the moist earth, and the azure sky—
Till Bill, the last man in the world to dream,
  Murmur'd—" How still, how silent all things lie—
Upon my word, I quite romantic seem !
  So bedward to the tavern let us hie—
Or I shall lose my genius commercial
And take to star-gazing like you or Herschell."

LXXXI.

" Agreed," I answered—so we wended back
  Our pleasant way beneath the moon and stars,
Admiring many an object on our track,
  The pointed rocks *here* glistening like spars—
And *there* upon our vision frowning black
  Like castles ruin'd in our civil wars,
The river's sweeps—its gambolings. its eddies ;—
Until we thought—" how comfortable bed is ! "

LXXXII.

We reach'd the tavern—took a pipe and glass—
  The landlord kindly gave us his society,
A pleasant hour we contriv'd to pass,
  And cheerful grew—but not beyond sobriety—
We hit the medium—difficult, alas !
  'Twixt temperance and rabid inebriety—
We then our chambers gain'd, both neat and clean,
And soon were snoring the white sheets between.

LXXXIII.

Now at this break of action I must pause—
  My heroes I have fairly put to bed ;
And so I think, by all poetic laws,
  My muse may also rest her weary head—
Such is her will, which I obey, because
  Without her aid my inspiration's fled—
In Canto Third, I, ere I end, admonish you,
I'll tell you matters which will much astonish you.

END OF CANTO II.

CANTO III.

———

I.

WHY is it that we dream ?—does sleep produce
    Prophetic warnings of our future fate ?—
Or does the mind fantastically choose
    Visions, without a meaning, to create ?
I know not—Yet we read the ancient Jews
    Relied with much faith on the dreamy state ;
And Joseph gain'd his wondrous elevation,
Because of dreams he knew th' interpretation.

II.

Perchance our modern mode of dreaming's wrong,
    Or for it no interpreters we find ;
At all events our faith is not so strong
    In dreams as that which fill'd the Hebrew mind--
But still a frightful night-mare lingers long
    In our remembrance, and with undefin'd
Feelings of terror fills us—so intense
We scarce can rid us of their influence.

III.

However that may be—a troubled vision
    O'erpower'd my senses as in bed I lay—
To the beefsteaks perhaps would a physician
    Ascribe, that night, my fancy's varied play ;
And indigestion blame for the transition
    From scene to scene which led my mind astray—
All I can say is—rapidly before me —
Events were crowded after sleep came o'er me.

IV.

A gentle strain of music, sweetly stealing,
    Upon my rapt ear steep'd my soul in bliss—
Methought a fair girl, with much depth of feeling,
    A song was trilling in accord with this—
We sat together—the piano pealing
    With dulcet sounds that seem'd my ear to kiss—
'Twas Harriet's fingers harmony awaking,
Her ruby lips that warbling were making.

V.

And ever and anon she fixed her eyes
    That, 'neath their lashes beam'd with fondest love,
On mine—while sighs of passion did arise
    Which for free egress from my bosom strove ;—
And when the page's end I did surmise
    She'd reach'd, to turn it, promptly would I move—
Then, standing, I leant o'er her chair, approaching
My cheek tow'rds hers, that blush'd at my encroaching.

VI.

And then the music ceased ;—and, arm-in-arm,
    The instrument we left and stepp'd together
Upon a balcony—in no alarm
    Of interruption—It was glorious weather—
The sun shone brightly, and the zephyrs calm
    Would not have ruffled in their play a feather—
The broad St. Lawrence was majestic sweeping
Below—its ripples on our senses creeping.

VII.

And we convers'd in that low murm'ring tone
    So sweet to lovers, as we gaz'd around—
Our speech accompanied the waters moan
    In its low cadence, and by it was drown'd—
Our eyes with eloquent affection shone
    And clasp'd in dalliance, were our fingers found—
Since that first pair confess'd in Eden's bow'rs
Their mutual passion, was not love like ours.

VIII.

Then all was chang'd—Aloft with leaden hue,
    Frown'd on the storm-toss'd ship the lurid sky—
The howling winds across the waters blew
    Which all around us heav'd, as mountains, high—
A leak was sprung, and the despairing crew
    In drunken apathy prepared to die.
I thought my time was come—upon me broke
My Harriet's smile—I started and awoke.

IX.

I slept again—I was a wand'rer lone ;
    Forlorn and penniless I trudg'd along.
From lengthen'd fast my limbs were trembling grown
    And dark thoughts on my mind did wildly throng—
To rest my weary head I place had none
    So on the way sank down the stones among—
Losing a short time every trace of sorrow
As dreamless slumber did my senses borrow.

X.

But soon another vision fill'd my brain !
    I was reclining in a prison's cell—
Trying, without success, repose to gain ;
    And, on my fever'd ear, the midnight bell
Struck, and each sound produc'd a pang of pain—
    The agony that moment brought, to tell
No words are adequate—almost to madness
I was incited in my hopeless sadness.

XI.

E'en then an angel-face upon me loom'd
    Bidding my hot eyes moisten into tears,
And I, the accus'd one, and, perhaps the doom'd
    Wept with a joy that half dissolv'd my fears—
Sobbing I woke—the rolling thunder boom'd
    So loudly that it pain'd my startled ears—
I rose, and viewed while seated at the casement
A storm which shook the tavern to its basement.

XII.

'Tis no unusual thing, in that bright clime,
    For sudden thunderstorms to fill the sky.
The evening may be clear – at morning's prime
    To the rain's beat incessant may reply
The thunder rumbling with a din sublime,
    While the black clouds careering madly fly—
And the fork'd lightnings with effulgent play,
Shoot o'er the dark scene, ushering in the day.

XIII.

Such was the sight I gaz'd on, till my mind
    Of those fell dreams forgot the auguries.
The coolness of the atmosphere combin'd
    With the grand aspect of the warring skies
To calm my troubled spirit, and a kind
    Of sad yet pleasing feeling did arise
Within my bosom—the despair which crush'd
My soul had vanished, when the storm was hush'd.

XIV.

After I'd gain'd my bed, a gentle slumber,
    Replete with blissful visions, on me crept—
On lips and forehead kisses without number
    My love was pressing while entranc'd I slept—
How sweet a change from those transitions sombre
    Of dire events which, late, my thoughts had kept!
Then on a couch with Harriet I was seated
And my fond looks her eyes, love-beaming, greeted.

XV.

We were in England ;—and the time was Spring.
    The morning sun shone joyously without—
With the bird's warbling did the garden ring,
    Perch'd in the shrubs that grew the lawn about—
A pretty boy, in infant gambolling,
    Frisk'd on the floor, and sometimes, with a shout
Called his mamma—who then would turn away
And gaze delighted on her offspring's play.

XVI.

Then a loud rapping at the door assail'd,
    My ears unwilling, and the vision broke—
Incens'd to have my happiness curtail'd
    Methought I rose—In rising I awoke—
'Twas Bill, who me vociferously hail'd,
    Saying, "of six the clock was on the stroke"—
I rous'd myself, and from my bed I bounded
Just as the hour he had mentioned sounded—

XVII.

"Wait but a moment, and I'll ope the door,"
    I shouted; and my clothes began to don—
When the "Continuations" which I tore
    Where I had laid them, my eye glanc'd upon—
I paus'd aghast; admitting Bill before
    I struggled into them, resolv'd to con
With him some method for their prompt repairing
Ere we should start off for our morning's airing.

XVIII.

"Is there a tailor here?"—was my first query;
    "You see to what condition I'm reduc'd."
Said Bill, "your case is pitiable, very—
    And you must lie there till a needle's us'd;
So 'tween the sheets again your carcase bury,
    While I seek aid."   Half angry, half amus'd,
To bed I crept, and Bill the chamber quitted,
Taking my trousers to have them refitted.

XIX.

He soon return'd—no tailor he could find,
    But with the servant-girl he had contracted
For the repair; and half-an-hour assign'd,
    In which the business was to be transacted—
Then to partake of breakfast we design'd
    And travel where Bill's lady-love attracted.
The sun was shining bright—the Buggy mended
In the inn-yard its occupants attended.

XX.

Meanwhile we freely join'd in conversation.
   Anticipating a delightful day —
Until the girl the torn " continuation "
   With some skill mended at the door did lay—
The tap was cheering, and with animation,
   My bed I sprung from, casting sloth awaɣ,
I cloth'd my legs—with borrow'd razor shav'd,
And then my hands and face, as usual, lav'd.

XXI.

I quickly dress'd—the cleanly stairs descended,
   To join Bill who already was below,
I found him where with glee he superintended,
   The cooking of the breakfast—and a glow
From the hot stove, with nature's colour blended,
   Made his broad cheeks more rubicundly show—
He held with fork a beefsteak raw and juicy,
And carroll'd gaily, " Take your time Miss Lucy."

XXII.

" I'll take a walk, till you have done your cooking,"
   I said—and left him busily engag'd ;
I saunter'd out, into the stable looking
   At our steed, who his appetite assuag'd ;
. And then my mind inaction tame ill-brooking,
   I went to see what weather it presag'd.
Upon the Humber's bank I soon was pacing
And with enquiring glance th' horizon tracing.

XXIII.

It was a glorious morning—the bright sky
   Expanded o'er earth, like an azure dome.
The forest smil'd and frown'd alternately.
   Where the glad sun its vistas did illume
The foliage laugh'd—but where no beam could pry
   Sombre it was with a funereal gloom—
The joyous birds flitting on active pinions,
Shook off the moisture caught from their dominions.

XXIV.

The clearings too were pil'd with stouks of corn,
  Their gold contrasting with the forest's green,
And, here and there, as jocund as the morn,
  Scythes-cradled plying mowers might be seen.
Yonder, a field the landscape did adorn
  As yet uncut, the lofty woods between—
Where the full ears scarce felt the zephy'r sighing,
As vainly it to ruffle them was trying.

XXV.

And in the pastures—(brownish was their hue!)
  The lazy oxen, ruminating lay,
And with distended udders homeward drew,
  The cows impatient ; for, at early day,
Their liquid burden they should yield they knew,
  And wonder'd why the milk-maid stay'd away—
From each farm-yard, as forth he strutted, clear
The cock's shrill clarion fell upon the ear.

XXVI.

And after him his feather'd beauties came,
  Admiring seemingly his plumage bright ;
All his attention emulous to claim,
  Appearing jealous at a fancied slight ;
The smoke arose, where the fresh kindled flame
  In many a hut dispell'd the chill of night ;
And scarce exceeded, each ascending vapour
That which is caus'd by an expiring taper.

XXVII.

So clear the air was—not a trace remain'd,
  Of that dark storm which had obscur'd the sky
At early morning ; and my eyes I strain'd
  Vainly the smallest cloudlet to descry ;
A tiny rapid I had just attain'd,
  Where over rocks the stream rush'd foaming by—
When me approached an Indian squaw and maiden,
With fancy articles of bead-work laden.

XXVIII.

They were a contrast.   With her bright black eyes
     The girl stood smiling, and her wares displaying,
And me to buy did prettily advise,
     The pearls within her parted lips betraying—
Her nose was aquiline, of moderate size,
     And dimples on her roseate cheeks were preying—
Her chin was finely form'd—her *tout ensemble*
Was such as on you do not often stumble.

XXIX.

Tho' purely Indian, her complexion seem'd
     Scarce deeper in its hue than many a maid
Of Europe's daughters would have lovely deem'd,
     And, p'rhaps with art to rival have essay'd :
Her long black hair upon her shoulders stream'd
     No covering did its raven tendrils shade ;—
Graceful her form—her race alone confessing
Her mode of walking and her style of dressing.

XXX.

She wore a flimsy petticoat of cotton,
     So short t' have seen it prud'ry would have swoon'd—
Gay was its pattern, which I have forgotten,
     But in bright colours round her it festoon'd—
In mocassins of deer skin she did trot on
     Which legs and feet preserv'd from many a wound,—
And where with sinews these, her boots, were lac'd
The bead-work borders shew'd the lady's taste.

XXXI.

A piece of broadcloth, like a blanket shaped,
     Was o'er her shoulders flung, and reached her feet,
While from its folds her tiny arms escap'd—
     Upon her bosom did its corners meet ;
And were together by some process drap'd,
     So subtile it my scrutiny did cheat—
With her mamma, the daughter having painted,
I, gentle reader, will make you acquainted.

XXXII.

I scarcely need inform you she was old—
　　In her young days perhaps she had been handsome ;
But woman's care as years had o'er her rolled,
　　From ugliness had fail'd her face to ransom—
Now wrinkles marr'd the smoothness of its mould—
　　And teeth to lose already she'd began some.
The storms of passion round her mouth had traces
Left, as with dames of her age oft the case is.

XXXIII.

Her dark eyes gleam'd with an intense ferocity—
　　No love was lurking in their jetty balls.
She seem'd as if, in actions of atrocity,
　　And all that human nature most appals,
She had forgotten that impetuosity
　　Of heart which kindly sympathies recals—
And, for my custom, while she was appealing
My body thro' there crept an icy feeling.

XXXIV.

In costume she resembled much her daughter ;
　　But it was not so tastefully arrang'd.
The wish to please, which once her sex had taught her
　　Into contempt for outward show was chang'd :
For time a wild Philosophy had brought her
　　That her from woman's habits had estrang'd—
Her air its mistress studied to profess,
A female cynic of the wilderness.

XXXV.

The twain a pair of mocassins had sold me,
　　And them I was examining with care,
When us approach'd (the younger woman told me)
　　Her sire, an Indian of imposing air.
Polite he bow'd, as joyous to behold me ;
　　And in our conversation took a share—
A mien of court'sy I assum'd to greet him,
Myself professing gratified to meet him—

XXXVI.

His form was graceful and his stature tall,
  His limbs than strength display'd more of agility—
He was not what we Europeans call
  Of great force muscular ; yet with facility
The rifle that upon his arm did fall
  He wielded, intimating full ability
To raise it, should a foe or game require it,
And, with sure aim, at either promptly fire it.

XXXVII.

A blanket o'er his naked shoulders cast,
  Them scarce protected from the morning chill.
His broad chest tann'd by many a winter's blast
  Was bare and on it was tattoo'd with skill
A figure, emblem of some action past,
  Which, were it known, would make the warm blood thrill,
And from which he, perchance, a name had gain'd
Amongst his people, that the deed explain'd.

XXXVIII.

A pair of cotton drawers were loosely tied
  About his middle, reaching to his knees,
Where mocassins of plain untann'd deer-hide
  His legs protected from the storm and breeze,
And to his feet the want of shoes supplied
  So that, 'mid stones and shrubs, he walk'd at ease—
His long black hair he wore—an innovation
Upon the ancient customs of his nation.

XXXIX.

The white man's habits had produc'd a change
  E'en in that noble savage : and the lock—
The scalp-lock he did erst with care arrange
  To wave defiance in the battle's shock,
Was now discarded.   So does Time estrange
  From the most cherish'd customs man—a block
Hewn into shape by ages—and the wild
Indian to peaceful arts is reconcil'd.

XL.

In a broad belt which pass'd around his waist,
    There lurk'd a knife whose blade a sheath conceal'd ;
And a small hatchet, on whose handle trac'd
    Were figures, only partially reveal'd.
The former tho' its keen edge lay encas'd
    And peaceful there, could serve as sword and shield,
When in the battle or the chase it gleam'd,
And, from its stroke, a crimson current stream'd.

XLI.

His features, like his squaw's and daughter's, were
    Form'd in a Roman contour; and his eyes
Now shone sedate, and now, with savage glare,
    Roll'd like a Tiger's, when with spring he flies
Upon his victim.   I have said his air
    To me was gracious; and in his replies
To my enquiries he spoke most mournfully—
Yet seem'd to view the white man's labours scornfully.

XLII.

His rifle-butt he sank upon the ground,
    And the long barrel he did firmly grasp,
As furtively he threw a glance around ;—
    And still more firmly did his fingers clasp
It while he gaz'd, as if he something found
    Which mov'd him, like the stinging of an asp;—
And o'er his face the shadow of emotion,
Pass'd like a cloud above the sunlit ocean.

XLIII.

Short converse there we held ; and then we parted—
    He, with his squaw and daughters, turn'd away
Tow'rds the not distant forest, and I started
    Back to my breakfast, listlessly to stray;
And sad thoughts clung to me when they'd departed—
    Musing, I left my feelings to their play,
Which prompted melancholy cogitations
On the destruction of the Indian nations.

E

XLIV.

" His fathers o'er this country rul'd supreme,"
   Thought I—" ere the encroaching stranger came—
And the dense forests, then unfell'd, did teem
   For him with ev'ry species of game ;
The finny tribes, too, frolick'd in the stream—
   A banquet—he, at any time, might claim ;
Now fields and pastures by the white man clear'd,
Mock his dim eye, which once the wild woods cheer'd.

XLV.

" Without cessation, onward rolls the din
   Of the remorseless axe the stranger wields,—
Ever employ'd *his* darling trees to thin,
   Leaving their black stumps in the expanding fields—
And if a virgin wilderness to win,
   Westward he flies—his flight no long-time shields
Him from the havoc which the ' pale-face' makes,
When on the red-skins' hunting ground he breaks.

XLVI.

" And where a hundred tribes exulting, fill'd
   The forest vistas with their joyous shouts,
Scarce one is left.   The rest are fled or kill'd
   In border warfare with the Yengeese scouts ;
Where burn'd the watchfire the rich glebe is till'd,
   And, as each year returns, the corn-blade sprouts ;
While solitary red-men wander lone
In the vast tracts, which claims a distant throne.

XLVII.

" The captive Jew, when he ' sat down and wept '
   By Babel's waters: and his haughty lord
Demanded why his idle harpstrings slept,
   And fail'd a tune of Zion to afford—
In vain the instrument, with cold hand swept,
   Responded to it not an echoing chord—
To sing Jehovah's praise his tongue refus'd,
While o'er his father-land, forlorn, he mus'd.

XLVIII.

"His fate was sad; but sadder far to roam,
  As does the Indian in his native land,
Nor scarcely find on its expanse a home,
  Tho' crowded cities all around him stand;
Well, with despondent feelings overcome,
  Of his fierce passions may be lose command;
And weaken'd by disease, and sunk in vice,
Expire, to drunkenness a sacrifice."

XLIX.

As these reflections did my thoughts employ,
  I wander'd back, unconscious of the hour;
When me arous'd the shouting of a boy,
  Who, looking for me, all around did scour.
"Breakfast is ready," cried this small envoy,
  "And t'other gemman does the steaks devour."
"All right," I answer'd—"I was just returning—
That it was breakfast-time from hunger learning.

L.

"So let us on."—Away the urchin scamper'd,
  Like a Canadian "Puck" in ragged clothes,
And no excess of them his freedom hamper'd,
  For on his way he went "with naked toes;"
My appetite was keen, nor to be tamper'd
  With, of a morning's saunter at the close.
So my young Mercury I swift walk'd after,
His flying form exciting me to laughter.

LI.

Soon I the tavern reach'd; and at the table
  Was Bill engag'd devouring his beefsteaks—
"Your walk," said he, "t'account for I am able;
  I know inaction frets the heart that aches."
"That's good," replied I, "from a man—unable
  To leave the circle charmed his lady makes,
Some miles around her, like a rock of magnet,
Drawn to her side as fishes in a drag-net."

LII.

"Well! Well! we're spooney's both; but breakfast's waiting,"
    He answer'd quickly, "and you must admit
'Tis better far to eat it, than debating
    To waste your precious time, not touching it—
So fall to work—instead of hesitating—
    There is a chair for you—why don't you sit?"
His kind request I instantly complied with,
And him in masticating beefsteaks vied with.

LIII.

Our breakfast ended, and our bill discharged,
    To start off on our journey we prepar'd ;
The landlord on the diligence enlarg'd,
    With which to have our spring restor'd he'd car'd :
We left the house, and where the Humber marg'd
    Upon the tavern-yard—with elbows bar'd
We found the hostler occupied in washing
    Our mended Buggy—with assiduous splashing.

LIV.

We saw the spring was firmly now secur'd ;
    And, to complete his work with all due speed,
The washer we persuasively adjur'd,
    As we were anxious onward to proceed—
To Bill he said " I've done, sir. Be assur'd
    Your horse I'll quickly from the stable lead—
In a few minutes all shall ready stand,
For you the trip to go on, you have plann'd."

LV.

Cried Bill " we'll have a cocktail at the bar—
    A parting glass demands our host's civility ;
And, after having lighted a cigar,
    We'll put to proof again our steed's agility ;
The house we're bound to is not distant far,
    But the roads are not formed with much ability."
" Agreed," was my response. Our host approving,
Said, " that we ought to pledge him before moving."

LVI.

Our morning draughts were speedily compounded,
　　And while the liquor bubbled in each glass,
The Buggy's clatter on the pebbles sounded,
　　As to the tavern door it round did pass.
" Your man has kept his word," said Bill, astounded,
　　" Beneath his feet he lets not grow the grass ;
Nor will we 'neath our steed's when once we've started,
And from our hospitable friend here parted.

LVII.

" Drink off your cocktail then, no more delaying,"
　　We did so—" now mine host we want a light,"
Resumed my friend, impatiently displaying
　　His mild Havanah, and with dextrous bite
The end removing—" There's our hackney neighing,"
　　Cried I ; " for going, he's in glorious plight ;
So, Bill, be quick—I care not now for smoking—
Really your tardiness is quite provoking."

LVIII.

" I'm with you," was the answer ; and we sallied
　　Forth to our vehicle, and mounted it.
The hostler held the horse, and with him dallied,
　　As with fierce eagerness he champ'd the bit.
" To be upset, we've an objection valid,"
　　Said Bill, as, reins in hand, he down did sit ;
" Therefore hold yet a moment while I settle
Firm in my seat, for he's a steed of metal."

LIX.

" Yes, Sir," the man replied, the arch'd neck stroking
　　Of the impatient quadruped, the while,
Which ever and anon caressed him, poking
　　His muzzle where that uncouth groom did smile.
" Now you may let him go," quoth Bill, invoking
　　Again the hostler in his usual style.
And off we went, behind the hamlet leaving,
Bent on the object of our jaunt achieving.

LX.

Along the high-road first our way extended—
   And, while on it, tremendous was the pace.
Upon our right-hand was the forest blended
   With frequent clearings, some of ample space
Upon our left, a belt of trees defended
   Was by a bank, forbidding us to trace,
Where, with its broad expanse, Ontario lay,
It's wavelets stirring the light zephyr's play.

LXI.

Of morning full three hours were before us,
   E're the hot sun would pour his noon-tide blaze
And, as our steed exulting onward bore us,
   The breeze refreshed us, having power to raise
The foliage where the boughs projected o'er us,
   Forming green bowers to our upward gaze.
Oh! more than earthly was that glad sensation,
Which quicken'd then my glowing heart's pulsation.

LXII.

And Bill was mov'd—for not a word he uttered
   For many minutes, but abstracted sat.
Breaking into soliloquy, he muttered,
   After a pause, as he arranged his hat,
" This is sublime—I really feel quite flutter'd."
   Then he turned to me, " Lovelier than that
Was landscape ever?"—pointing as he spake
Where an unwooded dell reveal'd the lake.

LXIII.

" It is indeed, replied I ;—and see, skimming
   Like a wild sea bird when she claps her wings
In ocean's brine, yon light skiff; and it's swimming
   To aid, I can observe the steersman flings
Himself from side to side, his craft thus trimming
   And now the corner of his sail he wrings,
For in the waves that gently round him surge,
He has contrived his canvass to submerge."

LXIV.

Now the broad lake again was lost to view—
    And nought but trees were seen on either hand.
Here the huge hemlock, like a giant grew;
    There, more umbrageous, did the beech-tree stand—
The maple, its broad leaves contrasting threw
    Towards the dark oak, which, as it stood, it fann'd;
And play'd the wood-pecker, with tap incessant,
His bill that made an echo not unpleasant.

LXV.

Along the highway, p'rhaps another mile,
    We held our course; then turning to the left
Where a cross lane did thro' the woods defile,
    We went more slowly, for in fearful plight
Was here the track uneven, and the style
    Of filling its deep ruts, Canadian quite;
For logs, a foot apart, had been employed,
So that the road was nicely " *corduroy'd.*"

LXVI.

'Twas well for us our spring had been repair'd,
    Or surely a breakdown had taken place;
Tho' leisurely we went, nor trouble spar'd,
    The smoothest surface we could find to trace,
We sunk, for its false semblance unprepar'd,
    In the loose soil which did our wheels encase.
Then we had one wheel lever'd up on high,
While t'other a deep rut was swallow'd by.

LXVII.

At last I said, " I've heard, Bill, of *rough-riding,*
    And this is it, indeed, in all perfection ;
I will descend, while you the horse are guiding,
    The ' trap' 'twill lighten—if you've no objection."
He answer'd, " None ;" and so I took to striding,
    And he, by frequent changes of direction,
The ruts to shun made effort—often vainly,
While much I laugh'd at his progress ungainly.

LXVIII.

And then I him preceded. Here inclining
　　Down to a hollow in its undulation
The road was form'd, declivity combining
　　With each its other harassing vexation.
I reach'd the bottom ; and was just resigning
　　Myself—forgetting Bill—to contemplation,
When his loud shout recall'd me from my study—
One wheel was jamm'd fast in a pit-fall muddy.

LXIX.

Around us spread a cedar-swamp; and rotten
　　Was th' undersoil o'er which the road was carried—
This circumstance by Bill had been forgotten,
　　Or with more care the stoppage he'd have parried :
But seeing all was level, he, to trot on,
　　Made an attempt, which failing, there he tarried—
The last night's shower had madefied the quag-mire,
And, on his wheel, was acting as a drag, mire.

LXX.

" Here we are fast again," cried Bill, as lugging
　　At the encumber'd wheel, which would *not* move,
He rais'd his head, and pausing from his tugging,
　　Invited me to aid him it to shove.
" Here goes," quoth I ; and joined him in his hugging,
　　Until we rais'd it the soft mire above.
" Well done," said he ; " the horse I'll lead till clear of
The swamp, and such deceitful mud holes steer off."

LXXI.

" Nobly resolved," I answer'd, and proceeded
　　To take a survey of the place around—
The boggy soil and water me impeded
　　From ingress, so an eminence I found ;
And there, with careful scrutiny, I heeded
　　The shrubs that with unfading verdure frown'd—
The view was dismal, and the smell offensive,
Proceeding from an area so extensive.

LXXII.

The pitchy water bubbled up between
     The cedar stems, their lower branches laving,
And their gnarl'd roots might here and there be seen
     Like twisted adders the bright sunshine braving;
And long, rank weeds and flags did intervene,
     In the light breeze with gentle motion waving.
By an old snake-fence was the swamp surrounded,
And the broad forest the whole prospect bounded.

LXXIII.

From this I turn'd, and followed Bill, who, toiling
     Along the way, but little progress made,
I reach'd him quickly, and, together moiling,
     The perils of the morass to evade,
We managed—the good clothes a little spoiling,
     In which that morning we had been arrayed.
And soon we found a very great improvement
In the road's surface, quickening our movement.

LXXIV.

" And now," said I, " I think we'd better ride—
     A most unpleasant morning's walk we've taken.
" We will," as he his steed check'd, Bill replied,
     For here our chance is less of being shaken;
So then ourselves we seated side by side,
     After my friend the whip and reins had taken.
Along we jogg'd, until the lane was ended,
When turning to a plank-road we ascended.

LXXV.

" Now we are almost there," as swiftly rolling
     Over the even planks we made our way,
Cried Bill. " How easily our wheels are bowling
     Over these boards propitious to their play !
'Tis like the rail, save that instead of coaling
     Our engine, we but lash our bonny bay ;
See the farm-houses stand in many a clearing,
Shewing a settled district we are nearing."

LXXVI.

" Bill !" exclaim'd I, " assume your smile most winning,
   For soon you'll gaze upon your charmer's eyes,
And there is nothing like a good beginning
   In those affairs where beauty is the prize ;
Arrange your thoughts, too, while along we're spinning,
   And a good store of compliments devise.
Pray, tell me, aren't you nervous ? just a trifle,
Be candid—nor your inmost feelings stifle ?"

LXXVII.

" Not I," he answer'd, " I'm none of your sighers,
   I speak my sentiments, and if I find
The lady coldly looks on my desires,
   Her want of taste I pity, and resign'd,
The next I try whose face my fancy fires,
   Hoping to me she'll not prove so unkind ;
Altho' my flame at present is Miss Horner,
Were she to frown upon me, I would scorn her.

LXXVIII.

" And yet I love her—but I have not told her
   The state of my affections ; tho' she guesses
From my eyes' eloquence when I behold her,
   The hidden weakness which my heart confesses ;
To-day, however, I shall make a bolder
   Effort. and formally pay my addresses—
All I am anxious for's a fit occasion,
On which to tell her of my admiration.

LXXIX.

" You take the father—there's a jolly fellow,
   While the fair daughter does my care employ ;
He's been an officer, and is as yellow
   As any guinea you have seen, my boy.
With his campaigns in India, like Othello,
   He will incessantly your ears annoy.
But have a little patience with his weakness,
And, some day, I'll repay you for your meekness."

LXXX.

"Agreed," said I, "but whose is the house yonder,
    Standing conspicuous on a gentle hill;
See, round it, pastures, in which idly wander
    So many cows ;—and some are grazing still,
While others, ruminating, seem to ponder,
    Of the rich herbage having ta'en their fill;
See, too, how neatly are repair'd the fences,
It is a paragon of residences.

LXXXI.

"And young trees here and there in front are planted,
    And from the entrance there's a kind of sweep ;
A garden too, with inclination slanted,
    To catch the sun, where rose-trees layer'd creep
Down to the streamlet's margin, as if they wanted
    To taste its waters as below they leap.
I little thought so nice a place to meet with,
Beauty of scene and comfort so replete with."

LXXXII.

"That's where we're going," replied he, coolly—tight'ning
    His reins, and bidding me undo the gate.
T'obey him I jump'd down, and quick as lightning,
    It open'd—when he drove in at a rate
That to the house soon brought him, somewhat fright'ning
    Me, whom there *planté* he left to my fate—
Following, for his desertion I impeach'd him,
And as he hammer'd at the door I reach'd him.

LXXXIII.

A woolly head and ebon face appearing
    At the revolving door, I paus'd from speech,
That Bill of "¡Blackey" might obtain a hearing,
    And profit by the things that he should teach.
"Where is the Major?" asked he—"In de clearing,"
    The "Nigger" answer'd, with a grin to each—
"And Mrs. Horner, and Miss Bella?"   "Sitting
In de best parlour you'll find Missey knitting.

LXXXIV.

" And berry pleas'd to see you, Massa Duncan,
    Will Missey Bella be; and in de dairy
Is Misses," answer'd " Snowball," and he slunk in,
    The groom to call, of work superfluous chary ;
There then we waited, till, with aspect drunken,
    And slouching gait, but eye alert and wary,
Approach'd us an old man, our hackney taking,
Touching his cap—but never silence breaking.

LXXXV.

As " Blackey " had absconded, exploration
    Was requisite, and so we went within—
At the room-door we tapp'd, an intimation
    It was our wish an entrance there to win.
" Who's there ?" In gentle tones the exclamation
    Saluted us thro' that partition thin.
" 'Tis only I," said Bill, the handle turning,
And in we walk'd, his lady-love discerning.

LXXXVI.

She was a charming girl. Her golden tresses
    Flow'd o'er her neck of alabaster hue—
Her pouting lips seem'd moulded for caresses,
    And her bright eyes were liquid orbs of blue ;
Dazzling was her complexion, and your guesses
    At her smiles' meaning never would be true.
Her nose *un per retroussé* made quite piquant
Her face whose change of aspect was so frequent.

LXXXVII.

Kindly she welcom'd us, and me presented
    Bill.   Then he hung enamour'd o'er her chair ;
Nor of the views with which he came repented,
    While chain'd his sparkling eyes that vision fair ;
For ever, in sweet dalliance, contented
    Would he have stay'd with that bright maiden there.
But her mamma arriv'd, and having greeted us,
Demanded if our hackney had unseated us.

LXXXVIII.

" Why do you ask that question ?" Bill replied.

     " Because your clothes with mud are so bespattered,"
Was her response. " You'd better get them dried

     And brush'd ; and, see, your coat's a little tatter'd—
Bella shall mend it, while you are supplied

     With lunch." Bill answer'd " that it little mattered—
'Twould do ; and that the mud had us impeded,
Clogging our wheels, which pulling from it needed."

LXXXIX.

" However, we'll get brushed, and then return——"

     " But leave your coat," persisted still the lady ;
And Bill complied ; beginning so to learn

     T' obey in small affairs he must be ready.
" Now to get Adonised be our concern,

     Then for the luncheon we are promised," said he.
The room we left, at this, and to the stable,
Clothes-brush in hand, we took our valet sable.

XC.

And there he scrap'd us well, and brush'd us clean,

     Excepting where adhesive, yet the mire
Was moist as ever it at first had been,

     Needing to harden it the aid of fire ;
The kitchen stove we went to, and did lean,

     Drying our clothes there till we did perspire.
The nigger roll'd his saucer eyes and giggl'd,
As round the place with uncouth gait he wriggl'd.

XCI.

His wife, too, chatter'd with her lord and master,

     And pester'd Bill to tell the comic tale,
How we had chanc'd to meet with our disaster,

     Nor ceas'd until she'd manag'd to prevail ;
And when he'd done so, wagg'd their tongues the faster.

     Then we made " Blacky" with his brush assail
The mud that was become quite dry and crusty,
And, as he groom'd us, fell in cloudlets dusty.

XCII.

We called for water next, and wash'd our faces
    And hands; and so for luncheon were prepar'd,
Having of travel freed us from the traces.
    "Now we must join the ladies," Bill declar'd;
"Just so," said I, "for not a stain defaces
    Our garments, so well has our valet car'd."
We gain'd the parlour.   Bill sat in a corner
With Bella, and I talk'd to Mrs. Horner.

XCIII.

'Tis strange mammas each other should resemble—
    They all wear caps and wigs and muslin tuckers,
And think, as parent rose-trees, they assemble
    Their daughters round them like so many suckers.
And so they do, for at *their* thorns we tremble,
    When of their offspring fair we would be pluckers;
Unless with riches we should be abounding,
When their attentions are almost confounding.

XCIV.

Now Mrs. Horner was a goodly sample
    Of the tribe motherly; yet not unkind—
To others she might offer an example,
    If each to her own failings were not blind;
She just curb'd Bill, but did not seek to trample
    Upon his feelings, without cause assign'd—
And so the lovers manag'd their flirtation
Much to their minds, while we held conversation.

XCV.

Bill was not a bad "Match."—For tho' not wealthy,
    He was deem'd steady; and his business paid;
Young too, of handsome form was he, and healthy,
    And had much knowledge of his line of trade;
I saw the mother many glances stealthy
    Cast tow'rds her daughter, which her thoughts convey'd—
And these were, "no such chance again may offer,
Accept him frankly, if his hand he proffer."

XCVI.

And then our sable friend brought in the tray
　　With viands fill'd, our appetites awaking—
So Bill was forc'd, tho' loath, to come away
　　From his fair lady-love, her side forsaking—
The mother having called him to display
　　His skill in carving while we were partaking
Of beef, and ham, and fowls, which late had flutter'd
At the barn-door, and cheese, and bread well butter'd.

XCVII.

The usual small-talk pass'd around the table ;
　　The elder dame expressing her regret
The Major, absence by, inexplicable
　　Was not permitted on us eyes to set—
But might we not, now we were comfortable,
　　Out on the farm to meet the laggard, set ?
Bella would guide us.　True, the day was warm,
But not oppressive, since the recent storm.

XCVIII.

It then was noon—the dinner-hour was four,
　　" The Major too would shew us the estate."
Bill wink'd at me ; and ere she added more
　　I said " we'd better do so than await
His coming—that I wish'd much to explore
　　The fields and woods I'd gaz'd on at the gate—
But, would Miss Horner go with us ?"　" With pleasure,"
She made reply, " when I shall be at leisure.

XCIX.

" But first, you know, I must complete your coat,
　　(Turning to Bill)—It will not take me long."
Down then she sat to work, and did denote
　　Her rapid stitching, she could not be wroug
In what she promis'd.　" Meanwhile I'll devote
　　A short time to the garden, and among
The flow'rs," I said, " I'll take a little airing,
While you, Miss Horner, are the coat repairing."

C.

And then I quitted them—the garden gain'd,
 And, turning down a walk, approach'd the stream—
The rose-trees on its bank were scarce restrain'd
 From bathing in its swift wave's varying gleam ;
But, coy, it shunn'd the contact, and disdain'd
 To kiss the Gul, the Persian poet's theme ;
And fled, escaping o'er a pebbly bar,
Like Joseph from the wife of Potiphar.

CI.

This I'd observ'd while we were on the road,
 Which the stream lav'd, but all its beauties then
I could not mark as well as now they shew'd,
 Brought closely home to my enchanted ken.
Backward and forward on the path I strode,
 And ever paus'd from promenading, when
I reach'd the point were stream and roses vied
To charm my eye—intensely gratified.

CII.

The bright parterres upon the lawn I view'd,
 Blooming with flowers beneath the midday sun,
Which cheer'd with joyous beam my solitude.
 There's was an elouquence I could not shun.
Each leaf, each bud, with language was endued,
 Preaching the glories of the Eternal one ;
And, rapt in thought, my soul expanded soar'd
From nature's loveliness to nature's Lord.

CIII.

" The last two lines are plagiarised from Pope !"
 The critic, frowning, will perchance exclaim.
I answer, " No !" and what I say, I hope,
 Will not tend my veracity to shame—
Surely, when to their feelings they give scope,
 To two men may arise ideas the same—
The thought was *Pope's*, now in my verse it shines ;
It sprang spontaneous, as I penn'd the lines.

CIV.

But to resume. Came o'er me the reflection
　I must re-enter and prepare for walking
As we'd agreed; and, at the recollection
　I turn'd, when on my ear there fell the talking
In low tones of the pair; and an objection
　Having a love-confession to be baulking,
I paus'd, and thro' the window an observer
Became of Bill and Bella's am'rous fervor.

CV.

He must have told her of his cherish'd flame,
　For round her waist his loving arm was flung,
And leaning on him was her shrinking frame.
　With downcast eyes upon his neck she hung.
Her glowing cheek confess'd her maiden shame,
　As to her lips her lover's, billing, clung.
" A pretty sight," thought I; "but they'll detect me"—
So off I went, for fear they should suspect me.

END OF CANTO III.

CANTO IV.

—

I.

The varied pleasures of the world I've tried—
    There is a gladness emanates from each,
But one occurs—to some alas! denied,
    Which novel feelings to the heart does teach.
Describe it! tho' my numbers smoothly glide,
    They cannot paint what beggars human speech—
Why do we mortals pant for heav'n above?
When almost heavenly's the first kiss of love.

II.

Whate'er may chance to be man's rank or fate,
    The peasant and the prince alike are blest,
When first the tale of passion they narrate
    To those by whom love also is confest—
No pomp or glory can so elevate
    The heart, or, with delight, so fill the breast,
As the low words a blushing maiden uses,
When she clings, trusting, to the man she chooses.

III.

Bill Duncan was as free from all romance
    As e'er in dry-goods and hard-wares was dealer.
The sole bent of his thoughts was to advance
    In the pursuit of wealth; and no appealer
To novels for fine fancies, where a glance
    From each sweet girl make some one long to steal her,
Was he—but still all conq'ring love beset him—
And maugre mental conflicts fierce upset him.

IV.

How he'd have laugh'd at me, was my reflection,
　　Had we chang'd places; and to him espial
Had chanc'd of my disclosure of affection :—
　　: How he'd have ask'd me, taking no denial,
" What words I used, how varied the complexion
　　Of my fair charmer in her hour of trial ! "
And shall not I now follow his example,
Twitting him also ?   There's occasion ample.

V.

" No ! " thought I to myself, " I'll be discreet
　　And rein my satire, 'twill be my turn next ;
I shall be always now prepar'd to meet
　　His banter—when by him I shall be vex'd—
And 'neath a tamarack I took a seat,
　　How to proceed exceedingly perplex'd—
I dare not join the lovers till abated
Their fondness somewhat was ; and so I waited.

VI.

Then of my own dear love, I pensive, mus'd.
　　Before my mental gaze her dark brown hair
In classic bands was tastefully diffus'd
　　Around her brow so delicately fair.
Her cheek was pale, as tho' it me accus'd
　　Of not being present, her pain soothing, there ;
And her white hand its symmetry display'd,
The soft chin pressing of the languid maid.

VII.

Her eyes were downcast ; but at times bright flashes
　　Of mellow radiance their orbs did display,
Making them shine within their silken lashes,
　　Till they encounter'd the sun's fiercer ray—
Which, with its pow'r, each milder gleam abashes,
　　And them, with curtain'd lids to hide their play
Compell'd.   She turn'd then with a look profound,
Emitting floods of light my heart that drown'd.

VIII.

"She is a lovely girl, indeed," I sigh'd.

   "Will Bill and Bella never have done kissing?
(Then Harriet's ruby lips in thought I ey'd)

   Surely, they'll seek me when they learn I'm missing."
To stay, or enter, I could not decide—

   The point was difficult, and—here a hissing
Rous'd me—I started, from the dread sound shrinking,
Fearing a snake had stol'n on me thinking.

IX.

I look'd around—erect my hair was standing,

   And a cold sweat was gathering on my brow.
But, as I'd understood, without commanding

   First your attention with his tail some-how,
The rattlesnake ne'er seiz'd his prey, unhanding

   Which I had grasp'd, when I arose, the bough,
I drew a long breath; and beyond the fencing
I saw the groom to clean our horse commencing.

X.

And it was he who made that startling sound,

   Which so had frighten'd me, to aid his scrubbing—
Hearing my sudden spring, he turn'd him round,

   Pausing a moment from his strenuous rubbing,
To see what in the garden would be found;

   Thinking, perhaps, a pig might there be grubbing.
At once he knew me, but spoke not, resuming
The hissing at the same time with his grooming.

XI.

I've often wonder'd why, by grooms, 'tis thought

   (And lads aspiring to the same vocation),
That in the way of cleaning horses, nought

   Can e'er be done, but the manipulation
To its perfection, doubtless, must be brought

   By the tongue's hiss, as if in emulation
Of the hand's work.   That all use this strange practice,
For philosophic minds a curious fact is.

XII.

"An odd man that," methought.　"He must be dumb,
　　Or else he has been school'd his tongue to bridle.
Perhaps his calling may have giv'n him some
　　Ideas of silence, so his speech lies idle.
I'll draw him out, nor will I be o'ercome
　　Till means of op'ning converse I have tried all."
So thro' the gate I went, and having reach'd him,
"To tell me what the time was, I beseech'd him."

XIII.

He did not hear me, or he took no heed
　　Of my enquiry; but continued brushing,
Mute as before, the sleek coat of the steed,
　　With the exertion his brown visage flushing.
I ask'd again, determin'd to succeed,
　　His elbow with my finger slightly pushing—
Dropping his brush, his watch he drew, which done,
He shew'd me on it, it was nearly one.

XIV.

"Our horse was warm, when we arriv'd this morning,
　　My friend," said I, t' elicit a response;
He nodded, every other answer scorning,
　　Nor ceas'd his wash-leather from using once.
"Were this man mine," methought, "I'd give him warning—
　　Did I not also rap him on the sconce."
Here Bill and Bella, in the yard appearing,
Took me to walk with them out in the clearing.

XV.

Slightly confus'd they look'd.　This observation
　　I made, but put no question to the pair;
I enter'd gaily into conversation,
　　Stating how much amus'd I had been there
With the groom who disdain'd articulation,
　　As if in words there lurk'd a hidden snare.
"He ne'er speaks," Bella said, "excepting when
Tipsy with whiskey, he's loquacious then!"

XVI.

"Had I a chance, I'd surely learn his story,"
    I answered; "but we're leaving you to-night;
Beneath those locks of his unkempt and hoary,
    There dwell the memories of many a fight
Against the cares of this world transitory,
    I'm sure his history would prove I'm right,
What do you think, Miss Horner?"   "Think as you do,"
Was her reply.—"He's seen what very few do.

XVII.

"But you'll not go to-night, for William has
    (And, at the name, how glowing the suffusion
Of crimson, rising to her sweet cheek was
    The tell-tale hue of modesty's confusion!)
Some business which will occupy papa's
    Attention long to bring to a conclusion—
So you must stay with us until to-morrow.
Of your time so much we may surely borrow."

XVIII.

"I had a special reason for returning
    This evening," I in my turn, blushing stammer'd;
"But since you press me, I don't mind adjourning
    My business for a day."—At Bill, enamoured,
I cast a glance, with indignation burning;
    And, 'gainst his plan of staying, would have clamour'd,
But Bella's presence from complaint restrain'd me,
Tho' much indeed the disappointment pain'd me.

XIX.

And then she led us through the pastures 'till
    We gain'd a grove of maples, at whose roots
The little juice-troughs were remaining still—
    Made to receive the sap, which upward shoots
Within each stem in spring—a luscious rill,
    That trickling gently from its source, salutes
The settler's eye—delighted—who well knows
When the sap rises will depart the snows.

XX.

We stop'd, the young trees' pleasant shade enjoying—
    The graceful foilage in the light air wav'd,
Which, with the broad leaves amorously toying,
    Seem'd there to linger, by delight enslav'd—
And Bill, the while, each winsome art employing
    Towards his fair charmer lovingly behav'd,
Whereas I felt myself *de trop* and lonely,
Thinking of Harriet and her ancle only.

XXI.

At last Bill said—" 'Tis useless standing here,
    Where shall we find the Major ?"   " In the field
Beyond the sugar-bush (and we are near),
    In which their cradl'd scythes the mowers wield."
Bella replied, " He'll certainly appear—
    For he is dubious of his harvest's yield."
" Come, Bella," then quoth Bill, and they proceeded,
Leaving me there alone, in thought, unheeded.

XXII.

A little dapper military man
    Arous'd me from my day-dream, as he hurried
To where I stood absorb'd.   He almost ran,
    So swift his pace was; and his air was flurried.
And now he doff'd his straw-hat, and began
    To wipe his head—in his bandana buried;
And now, with nervous hand, his white blouse twitching,
He seem'd to feel his little body itching.

XXIII.

And then he cast an anxious look around—
    His grey eye flashing, as if something seeking
On which to vent the fury that he found
    Within his bosom, and which kept him reeking.
His meagre face, by many a summer brown'd,
    Long years in eastern climates spent, bespeaking,
Shone in the sun like oil-skin, and was sprinkled
With dewy sweat-drops on its surface wrinkled.

XXIV.

He must have been (I thought) at least three score
 (I'm anything but skilled at guessing ages),
His years, however, jauntily he bore,
 Like those just entering manhood's earlier stages;
And the conviction ne'er his mind came o'er
 That of life's book he'd reach'd the latter pages.
Bill Duncan's friend, the Major, thus I judg'd,
As tow'ds me, in my solitude, he trudg'd.

XXV.

"A glorious morning! is it not? by Jove—
 I'm glad to see you, sir, on my poor farm;
My wife has me informed that Duncan drove
 You hither with him to enhance the charm
Of his society. How can I prove
 My ardent wish your *ennui* to disarm?
I've just been to the house to fetch some whiskey,
The day's so bright and warm, I feel quite friskey.

XXVI.

"It was a day like this when we assail'd,
 Under old Lake, the fort of Alighur—
I was an ensign then, and never quail'd
 When duty call'd me—but I will defer
My tale till evening. Many a mother wail'd
 The son, who on that day was lost to her."
Thus spake he quickly, as he stood there gasping,
And with his fingers he my hand was clasping.

XXVII.

"But where are Duncan and Miss Horner?" "Gone
 To look for you, sir, in a field hard by,"
Replied I, as he plac'd his bottle on
 The ground, and once more did his forehead dry.
"Thither I'm bound," said he, "they've nearly done,
 But you shall see my lab'rers as they ply
Their cradled scythes. I've three at work to-day, sir.
We farmers find this harvest-time no play, sir."

XXVIII.

And off he bustled ; and I had to follow
    As best I might; so, keeping him in view,
I left the sugar bush, and in a hollow,
    Where nought but cherry wood and hickory grew,
I came up with him, skimming like a swallow
    Over the ground uneven.   When I drew
Near him, he shouted, " You're an able walker,
Perhaps a Scotchman, and an old deer-stalker."

XXIX.

" No, sir, I'm English ; and have never been
    In Scotland," said I, " to my deep regret ;
But my own land contains full many a scene
    To charm the eye, where I've my footsteps set.
With such, in shady lanes, and pastures green,
    Pedestrianising, I have often met."
" Ah! Ah! a merchant, and have left your desk
To wander in search of the picturesque."

XXX.

"'Tis true, indeed, I've been a merchant, Major,
    At least commercial was my education ;
But you're by no means a correct presager,
    In thinking I forsook my former station
For travel, bitten by romance"—" I'll wager
    It was ill-health that chang'd your destination
In the pursuits of life."   He answer'd quickly.
" You left the office because you were sickly."

XXXI.

" You've hit the truth," said I, " my health had fail'd me.
    For business I had ne'er the least distaste,
And with inaction fretting, there assail'd me
    An ardent wish to travel—nor to waste
My youthful days at home ; so I avail'd me
    Of the first chance that in my way was plac'd,
The beauteous scenes of my own land to visit;
Which done, I'm here—the plan's no bad one, is it ?"

XXXII.

" A good one, certainly, and I admire
    Your spirit in adopting it; you'll see
Much of the world; and if you should desire
    Your business after to resume, will be
More capable; the knowledge you acquire
    From many a prejudice will set you free.
No mean advantage; for distorts the mind
Ignorance when with prejudice combined."

XXXIII.

He look'd oracular, while he was giving
    This, his opinion, and assum'd a dignity
Of air, which suited him of all men living
    The least, and with it a sublime benignity
In his expression, his whole face retrieving
    From its accustom'd aspect of malignity—
I could not keep from laughing, for so funny
He seem'd to me—No, not for any money.

XXXIV.

He star'd at me, and ask'd me why I smil'd.
    I pointed where a ground-squirrel was running,
Now in our path, now round the trees—its wild
    And tim'rous nature having taught it cunning.
It shew'd its sleek skin with the pride a child
    Will oft evince a new suit after donning.
" Ah," said he, at the pretty creature glancing,
" Had I my gun here I'd soon spoil your dancing."

XXXV.

And soon we reach'd the field.   The Major panting
    Drew near the couple, and took Duncan's hand,
Then from his bottle hastily decanting,
    Into a horn that on the ground did stand,
Some whiskey—for the water which was wanting,
    He issued to a mower his command
To go down to the brook, whose murmur distant,
Invited the approach of his assistant.

XXXVI.

Meanwhile the two most gallantly were mowing—
    One was a Scotchman—Irish was the other:
Their cradled scythes around the bright straw throwing,
    They laid it in rows on our common mother—
An eager look the whiskey on bestowing
    With an impatience that they could not smother,
To quench their parch'd lips with it, when diluted—
A beverage to their taste and labour suited.

XXXVII.

" Arrah !" said Pat, when they the swathe had ended,
    " Major, I'd like that whiskey to be dhrinking,
This is dthry work, and would be much amended
    With, of the ' crater ' just a dthrop, I'm thinking—
Give us a taste, your honour ; it looks splendid ;
    And, with a burning thirst I'm well-nigh sinking—
The boy you sent for wather now is near us,
Some whiskey, Major, darlint, then to cheer us."

XXXVIII.

" Don't be so tiresome, Pat, and you shall have it.
    Lay down your scythe, and speedily come to me.
The whiskey is, I'll take my affidavit,
    True *Bush Mills*.   From a man that wouldn't jew me
'Twas bought ;—so well your Irish throat may crave it—
    'Tis glorious liquor, or may ill beshrew me.
Your Scotch friend also ' Mountain Dew ' will tipple,
As if he suck'd it from his mother's nipple."

XXXIX.

Thus spake the Major, as the third man brought
    A pitcher full of water from the brook,
Which from his grasp the vet'ran, quick as thought,
    To mix the grog for his friend Paddy took ;
Who, the refreshing draught, when mingled, caught
    In his right hand, with a triumphant look,
And rais'd ; his nose into the vessel dipping,
Its rim the while affectionately lipping.

XL.

Then both the Scotchman and "the boy" who ran
    For water, afterwards assuag'd their thirst
And to his work again each sturdy man
    Applied himself, with all the vigour erst
He had display'd, pursuing the same plan
    Of mowing as when we upon them burst.
Their master ey'd the trio most complacently,
And Paddy said they did their business "dacently."

XLI.

We left them moiling still, our steps retracing
    Along the path we'd come—the Major leading;
His conversation, as we walk'd, embracing
    Tales of his youthful exploits—some exceeding
Belief, and from my memory effacing,
    By their astounding marvels, all from reading
I'd gather'd of the doings of Munchausen,
Whom fairly beat this old man when his war's on."

XLII.

When we had gain'd the house, mamma, all smiles,
    Receiv'd us, having doubtless seen her daughter
Since Bill, with all a lover's suasive wiles,
    To change her name, had earnestly besought her.
Drest was the matron in the best of styles,
    And having us'd, while we walk'd, soap and water
Her face to cleanse, a tinge of rouge applying,
She look'd more glaring, there was no denying.

XLIII.

Her hair, or rather the peruquier's, fell,
    In neat curls on the imitated rose,
Which, so *exotic*, in each cheek did dwell,
    That no one it could *natural* suppose,
Above a turban did sublimely swell,
    Compos'd of net-work, trimm'd with yellow bows
Her gown was purple satin, and the flounces
Weigh'd, from their size, I'm certain, sev'ral ounces.

XLIV.

"Major," said she, and wink'd upon her deary,
  "These gentleman with us will stay the night.
Their homeward road is hard to find and dreary—
  I'm sure you'll welcome them with much delight."
"I will," cried he; "for I've long had a theory ;
  That where you dine, to sleep is always right."
Then Bill informed the senior he desir'd
To have some speech with him ere he retir'd.

XLV.

"Come, then, my boys, your chambers I will show you,
  For Mrs. Horner doubtless has prepar'd
A couple, where, with comfort, you may stow you,
  And for your easy sleeping well has car'd."
She nodded, with an air that said "I know you
  Will be convinc'd I have no trouble spar'd
T' ensure you that repose which you'll find grateful—
To travellers a bad bed is always hateful."

XLVI.

So up the stairs the gallant vet'ran pass'd,
  And pointed out to each his crib for sleeping.
The chambers were not large, but might be class'd
  Among the cleanest I e'er saw—In keeping,
From 'neath the coverlets above them cast,
  To rest inviting, were the white sheets peeping.
Soon I was occupied with my ablutions,
Making, the while, most sturdy resolutions.

XLVII.

One of them was that Bill should not persuade me,
  Whatever pretext he might conjure up,
Longer to stay, then when with eve to shade me,
  The morrow should begin; but that I'd sup
At home—another was, if chance should aid me
  With the groom taciturn I'd take a cup,
So that I might obtain the man's strange history,
For he'd provoked me with his air of mystery.

XLVIII.

Whilst thus I mus'd, Bill sought me, in high glee,
    Anxious to tell me he had won his charmer.—
"She's mine," he cried, "and I have but to see
    The Major.   As his wife's already warmer
In her attentions—Pa will too agree.
    I was excited, but am getting calmer.
Eh ? What's the matter—you look dull and stupid!
I thought you were a votary of Cupid."

XLIX.

"Yes, so I am," I answer'd.—"That's the reason,
    While you are joyous, I am far from merry—
Were I to smile to love it would be treason,
    And you're considerate, my dear fellow, very,
Thus to prolong your visit out of season,
    When I'd as soon be in the wilds of Kerry.
'Tis sweet for you, no doubt, this constant cooing,
But recollect, I also, would be wooing.

L.

"To-morrow night I'll go—I'm fond of walking,
    Beside by moonlight would look grand the swamp.
I'm dying to return.—It's useless talking,
    To-morrow night I will most surely tramp,
You look as if you were intent on balking
    My wish (here I upon the floor did stamp),
On foot, I tell you, if not in your carriage,
I'll go.—You'll wish me next t'await the marriage."

LI.

"Well! Well! be quiet; and our leave we'll take
    To-morrow evening since you so desire,
Stay but till then," he answered, "for my sake,
    And tell me don't you Bella, much admire."
"I do," replied I; "and her beauties make
    My heart with thoughts of my own lady fire;
But I'll be patient till the time you mention,
As you'll not thwart of going then my intention."

LII.

So having made our bargain, we descended
   The stairs, and in the room the ladies found,
Where Bill and Bella love-sighs deep had blended,
   Telling each thought, unconscious that the sound
Of their half-whispering voices had ascended
   To my ears, as I stood without spell-bound—
Miss Horner wore a dress of muslin—blue—
And a pink sash contrasted with its hue.

LIII.

A well-assorted bouquet nestles in
   The azure folds which on her bosom press'd,
The flowers appearing just where did begin
   The sash's edge to gird their place of rest.
I thought (so thinking surely was no sin)
   The nosegay there must be supremely blest.
She blush'd as Bill approached—that blush outshone
The lovliest rose which bloomed above her zone.

LIV.

Except to lovers, Love's uninteresting.
   The game cannot be played by more than two.
A third's *de trop* to those love manifesting,
   Nor will a quartette at the pastime do.
A pair—when smitten—should—I'm far from jesting,
   Be therefore left together the day thro':
This mayn't be proper,—but accords with reason,
Let prudes the matter say just what they please on.

LV.

What is a man to do, or say, or think,
   A lady fair and her adorer present,
Who comfortably on a sofa sink,
   In conversation, leaving him, unpleasant
With an old prosing dame, who does not shrink
   From pestering him with questioning incessant;
" Who are his friends ?   His father ?—what profession
He has been bred to ?"—Must he make confession?

LVI.

Or must he snub her, and in silence sit,
　　Betraying that he really feels offended,
That she should try to wheedle, bit by bit,
　　His history from him in a strain where blended
An air of pity are, and strokes of wit,
　　(At least for wit the efforts are intended.)
His best plan is, I think, to laugh and flatter,
As if he really lik'd her tiresome chatter.

LVII.

This was the method I pursued when seated
　　With Mrs. Horner in a *tête à tête.*
I parried her enquiries, and defeated
　　All her attempts the veil to penetrate,
Which cover'd my condition—until heated,
　　Her fan she brandished at a furious rate,
Looking upon me with a kind of terror,
She'd thought me *young* and *green,* but saw her error.

LVIII.

I was delighted with her half-confusion.
　　I felt triumphant o'er my baffled foe.
Her face acknowledg'd plainly the delusion
　　She first had harbour'd did much fainter grow;
She was fast forming a correct conclusion
　　About my character—the truth was slow
In breaking on her, but at length had broken—
Her change of manner did the fact betoken.

LIX.

And when she spoke again 'twas to a man
　　Who knew the world—its principles of action—
The varied motives which inspire each plan,
　　Form'd for its interest by every faction.
To feel a reverence for me she began,
　　And what I said receiv'd with satisfaction
'Twas evident she thought me a most sensible
Young fellow—if I were more comprehensible.

LX.

Now, too, the Major join'd us, having chang'd

　　His dress since we had parted.　He appear'd

More like a soldier, his toilette arrang'd,

　　Than when his mowers he with whiskey cheer'd.

Colonial life had him somewhat estrang'd

　　From good society, at which he jeer'd,

Altho' he almost worshipped a new-comer,

Who, his heart gladden'd, as the breath of summer.

LXI.

This feeling, on his part, procur'd civility

　　To strangers who could give him information

How the world wagg'd, and if they had ability,

　　He welcom'd them, whate'er might be their nation ;

Living apart he mourn'd o'er the sterility

　　Of news, the effects of his long separation

From men and cities ; so a guest amused him—

After he'd gone the veteran abus'd him.

LXII.

Thus each arrival was to him the kind

　　Of mental food which yields a morning paper—

We read the article, and if we find

　　To our opinion's point it does not taper,

We lay it down, to every merit blind,

　　And swear the writer's some insolvent draper,

Or other tradesman, who his shop has quitted

To write on politics in strain half-witted.

LXIII.

'Twas thus the Major treated me and others ;

　　He learn't our feelings—everthing about us,

Behaving as if all there met were brothers,

　　And he could not a moment live without us ;

One would have thought he'd known our fathers', mothers,

　　Loving us so well that he would not doubt us ;

But, when our backs were turn'd, how chang'd, oh, Lord !

His tone was—all who'd left him he abhor'd.

G

LXIV.

I was, however, present,—what he thought
    I know not, and perhaps shall never know,
But me to fascinate, to bear he brought
    All his artillery of small-talk, so
That much I felt delighted, when I caught
    A glimpse of " Blackey," who did open throw
The door, exclaiming " Massa, dinner ready."
The Major led the way—I took the lady.

LXV.

I need not tell you, Bill of course contriv'd
    To give his arm to Bella.   I suppose
My readers are aware, before she's wiv'd,
    A man cling's to his love where'er she goes.
After their marriage, she must be depriv'd
    Of this support, as every party shows.
Why this should be so, I'm no able guesser,
'Tis strange a wife shuns ever her possessor.

LXVI.

The Major took his seat, and said his grace,
    And " Snowball" rais'd the cover from the dish,
The action preluding with a grimace.
    Appeared then black-bass—that most glorious fish !
Talk of your soles, eels, turbot, pike, or plaice,
    For none of these, would I, when hungry, wish
Had I a fresh black-bass, a full five-pounder
Tender as chicken, and than mutton sounder.

LXVII.

I never much admired the " gentle art,"
    And have not patience to become an angler:
Besides, with skill obtaining, one must start
    Which time requires enough to form a wrangler ;
And should long use dexterity impart,
    All ends in making one an idle dangler,
'Neath trees by streams, or else in punts on rivers.
    The very thought has given me the " shivers."

LXVIII.

In England, too, a man may fish all day,
　　And terminate his labours with a nibble.
This would appear to trifle life away,
　　Were its duration e'en what it is treble.
With precious time one can't afford to play,
　　I feel 'tis gliding from me whilst I scribble,
We've something better to fill up our leisure
Than the pursuit of *ennui* as a pleasure.

LXIX.

But in America, I've felt delight
　　With rod and line to take the finny tribe ;
The whole of the affair is diff'rent quite.
　　They are more plenteous than I can describe.
In rivers there they *will* be caught in spite
　　Of want of skill—It may be they imbibe
From being too numerous a desire to die,
And so despairing to the fish-hook fly.

LXX.

I know a spot where I've fish'd many an hour,
　　From early morning to the day's decline.
The river there leaps with resistless pow'r
　　Over the rocks unshapely, which combined
To form a rapid ; and deep channels scour,
　　Between the huge stones, where I drop'd my line.
I've taken many a Bass here, many a Dory,
Standing upon a wooded promontory.

LXXI.

But here the sparkling waters charm'd the eye.
　　Their roar was music to the listening ear ;
The foilage round me, and the azure sky
　　Above me—brightened by the sunshine clear—
These were companions—tho' no man was nigh,
　　And seem'd my solitary sport to cheer.
How different this from Walton's mooning mystery.
I always nod when I peruse his history.

LXXII.

Meantime while I'm employ'd on this digression,
    The lady sits behind the soup tureen,
Asking us all, with blandness of expression,
    Thro' the ascending vapours, dimly seen,
If we'll a plateful take, with much profession,
    That it compounded by herself had been.
" The servants here but cook the plainest dishes,"
She said, " and them not always to our wishes."

LXXIII.

Our hostess, with such candour having own'd
    The part she'd taken in the meal preparing,
'Neath which the board so hospitably groan'd,
    Of course some soup we took, ourselves declaring
Delighted with it—tho' her mate bemoan'd
    His hapless fate in such stuff to be sharing.
" The last you made, my dear," he said, " was better,
" And for that day's good meal, I was your debtor.

LXXIV.

" But this *Mock Turtle !* *Mock* it is indeed !
    I'd like to know extremely the ingredients
Forming the broth on which we're doom'd to feed.
    Many and skilful were, no doubt, th' expedients
You practised, to concoct it.   You may plead
    Our guests are pleas'd—they say so in obedience
To what they think politeness—I've observ'd 'em
Eating your strange production has unnerved 'em.

LXXV.

" Thus, Mr. Turnbull's emptied the decanter
    In vain attempts to wash your hodge-podge down.
If I don't ask him to take wine *instanter,*
    I know not what will—Nay, you need not frown,
Your soup will force him to be a levanter.
    Come, we'll its memory in Madeira drown.
It must be good—to my providing thanks !
For it has voyag'd, like Sir Joseph Banks."

LXXVI.

I took the wine with pleasure; for with water
    Myself I'd nearly deluged to redress
The soup's effects—It much resembled mortar,
    Save that of stiffness it had somewhat less;
And, Bella, in the very fact I caught her,
    Handed to " Blackey " her untasted mess,
While Bill, when of the wine her sire made mention,
    To drink some also signified intention.

LXXVII.

I think *his* soup he'd stoically swallow'd;
    Praise it he did—Mamma to gratify,
But a wink told me, ere the wine that follow'd
    Had reach'd his lip, the praise was all " my eye."
That vulgar phrase along the streets is halloo'd,
    Its derivation I cannot supply—
Just what I mean, however, it expresses,
Tho' with some plainness it my story dresses.

LXXVIII. ·

I was not sorry when a rump of beef
    Smok'd on the board beneath the Major's nose.
He ceased to scold, affording us relief.
    Such quarrels are, as every body knows,
Unpleasant, tending to destroy belief,
    That matrimony is exempt from woes:
I wonder parents, who have girls to marry,
Do not contrive such skirmishes to parry.

LXXIX.

And yet, oh human nature! thou art fram'd
    Of such perversities, thou wilt not bend
When policy demands it, tho' asham'd
    Are those whose tempers cannot condescend
To hide that passion which they should have tam'd,
    When the unseemly gush has reach'd its end.
I'm much afraid e'en to the close of time
The same thou'lt be in all, in every clime.

LXXX.

Here were a pair in the first gush of love,
 Too fond, perhaps, for logical deduction.
But the *scene* tended certainly to prove
 That anger to affection is destruction.
There was the Major, wroth as thund'ring Jove,
 Because the soup was nauseous in the suction,
And Mrs. Horner equally as furious,
Before their daughter, and her beau,—how curious!

LXXXI.

Surely such conduct gave Bill no impression
 From the excited senior had deriv'd
His charmer, that sweet virtue of concession,
 Which of her would a blessing make, when wiv'd.
And Bella's crimson'd cheeks implied confession,
 Her of all comfort had the *scene* depriv'd.
The Major was in fault,—he made a blunder,
Which might have put the turtle-doves asunder.

LXXXII.

But with the beef's arrival he became
 Much calmer; nay, he almost deign'd to smile.
The meat his temper had the power to tame,
 Its appetising odours calm'd his bile.
P'rhaps to himself he did his conduct blame,
 And so he ask'd each in the blandest style
To take a slice—our appetites to quicken,
While Mrs. H. was cutting up the chicken.

LXXXIII.

A couple were before her, in white-sauce
 Smothered; to carve them she refus'd my aid.
These dishes, with potatoes, form'd the course,
 And kidney-beans, between the two displayed.
I took a wing t' appease my hunger's force,
 As on Bill's plate some beef the Major laid;
Also a ham there was, I did not mention,
On a side-table, making no pretension.

LXXXIV.

And this the nigger carv'd, which spar'd us trouble.
  The table it would have too much encumber'd.
The wine again in every glass did bubble,
  Pour'd from decanters where its tide had slumber'd ;
In drinking which I had a duty double
  To do, as both the seniors I number'd
As my competitors—for Bill and Bella
Were close as two beneath the same umbrella.

LXXXV.

This course remov'd, pastry and sweets appear'd,
  Blanc mange, and tarts, and custards serv'd in glass.
Shapely the luscious edibles were rear'd,
  Tho' not conducive p'rhaps to health, each mass.
I took a custard, for the rest I fear'd
  Into my stomach down my throat to pass.
Some bread and cheese, of two descriptions follow'd,
All, save the soup, was first-rate that I swallowed.

LXXXVI.

The cloth was drawn ; the Major thanks return'd ;
  Enter'd our black friend then with the dessert,
And wines of various sorts, in coolers urn'd,
  Whose very sparkle made him look alert.
His master's temper he had fully learn'd,
  And knew he hated servitors inert ;
Thus was he made a butler quite superior,
If you forgot his very dark exterior.

LXXXVII.

The soldier now was really at his ease,
  And filled the ladies' glasses, then his own,
Passing the bottles that his guests might please
  Themselves.   The port was from the vintage grown
In *Thirty-four*, which the *gourmets'* decrees
  Amongst the best as yet produc'd do own;
Besides Madeira, Hermitage and Sherry
Were on the board to make the party merry.

LXXXVIII.

Our first glass was devoted to the Queen.
  One who had serv'd must hail with joy that toast.
This, our host's custom, long, each day, had been,
  For loyalty unshaken was his boast,
And, like the Cavaliers of old, I ween,
  He thought by drinking he evinc'd it most.
He gave no other—but in small talk mingled,
Shaking with laughter till the glasses jingled.

LXXXIX.

'Mong other subjects, Duncan mentioned horses,
  When to my thoughts recurr'd the silent groom.
I signified my wish of his discourses,
  To be a list'ner, should it be his doom
To rouse with liquor his colloquial forces,
  Removing from his brow the air of gloom
Which clung around it, while within the reach
I should remain of his well-hoarded speech.

XC.

The Major said, " to-night you'll have a chance,
  For when the harvest-men have done their labour,
And they have supp'd, each hero will romance,
  Striving with marvels to outshine his neighbour.
They'll whiskey have—which very circumstance,
  The tongue will loosen of old Adam Faber.
By ten o'clock—you may believe me fully—
He'll chatter like Demosthenes or Tully."

XCI.

" I'll join them then," I answered, " if you, madam,
  (Turning to Mrs. H.) have no objection."
" I've none," quoth she ; " your presence much will glad 'em,
  And they'll feel honoured by your predilection
For their society—I'm sure old Adam
  Will think of you in future with affection."
She stopp'd, and to her daughter nodded gravely,
Then, pompous, tow'rds the door she swept most bravely.

XCII.

And Bella follow'd—so we then remained
  T' indulge in our symposium together;
Our conversation was, at first, constrain'd,
  Touching upon the aspect of the weather,
Of which the Major, farmer-like, complain'd,
  (In this complaint are farmers "of a feather
All birds.")   We sat there, silent as the stars,
When our host rose and handed us cigars.

XCIII.

Which, when we'd lighted, and each man a cloud
  Of curling smoke emitted from his lips,
So that a hazy veil did all enshroud—
  We seem'd like planets under an eclipse.
Bill told the Major he should be "most proud"
  (Resting his hands, the while, upon his hips),
As soon as he could lend his ear in private,
A matter of some import to arrive at.

XCIV.

"Pooh! pooh!" the soldier answered, "not to-night.
  I never talk of business when I've dined.
I'm sure I am not now in fitting plight
  To your affairs, my friend, to bend my mind—
To-morrow morning I shall feel delight
  To listen to you if you're so inclined,
So pass the bottle, there's a jolly fellow,
To-day I am determined to get mellow."

XCV.

To do the Major justice, he evinced
  By his proceedings this determination—
He drank off bumpers constantly, nor winc'd
  From emptying each—in him was no evasion;
In my own mind, I long had felt convinc'd,
  His frequent draughts would tipsiness occasion;
I rather shirk'd the bottle, so did Duncan—
It would not do, with Bella, to be drunken.

XCVI.

After a pause, our host resumed the thread
    Of conversation from his haze of smoke,
Puffing the clouds in wreaths about his head,
    As he our long-continued silence broke.
" This morning, if I recollect," he said
    (His left hand thursting into his left poke,
While with his right he handled his cigar),
I made some mention of my deeds in war.

XCVII.

" We now are brought as 'twere to a dead lock
    In our discourse, so I'll resume the story—
The recollections that upon me flock
    Kindle anew my pristine thirst for glory.
I seem to feel again the battle's shock,
    And gaze, in mind, on many a carcass gory.
The fort of Alighur, I think, I mentioned.
For losses there was many a widow pensioned.

XCVIII.

" The fort was plac'd upon a lofty hill,
    Surrounded by a moat well filled with water.
A drawbridge swung, at the commandant's will,
    O'er this to there, in friendship, a resorter ;
To foes 'twas rais'd, constructed with such skill,
    It could be manag'd by a single porter.
At first appear'd the fortress inaccessible,
Which caus'd us disappointment inexpressible.

XCIX.

" But there had been a sort of terrace form'd,
    Filling the moat and bordering the wall.
From this we saw the stronghold might be storm'd
    And taken, if it taken was, at all.
Our blood with this discovery was warm'd,
    And we felt eager on the foe to fall—
Old Lake observ'd th' advantage, and decided
To seize th' approach this accident supply did.

C.

" To Colonel Monson the command was giv'n--
    I was an Ensign as, I think, I told you—
(At Cawnpore's fight I'd previously striv'n,
    Its tale at some time future I'll unfold you.
The natives under Perron there were driv'n
    Before our fellows, e'er I'd say ' behold you.')
The terrace we soon pass'd—the breast-work gain'd,
When by the wall impeded we remain'd.

CI.

" It was defended by a host of spearmen,
    Who, as we came, made desperate resistance.
Our soldiers were not in the mood to fear men,
    But for a moment there they kept their distance.
To escalade 'twas fruitless on to cheer men,
    So the artillery gave us assistance.
To burst the gate we sent for a twelve-pounder,
From the main-force where gunners did surround her.

CII.

" Before, however, we could point the piece,
    We were expos'd to a most galling fire,
Which never did a single instant cease,
    But caus'd full many a soldier to expire.
Our gallant colonel, whom no post did please
    But that where no one to the foe was nigher—
Was wounded at the opening of the action,
Retiring from it with dissatisfaction.

CIII.

" McLeod, the Major, to command succeeded—
    As brave a fellow as e'er drew a sword.
No greater efforts man could make than he did
    Speedy relief, with ordnance, to afford.
Meanwhile the native fire on us proceeded,
    Standing in an inaction we abhorr'd—
I felt myself, I do not mind confessing,
That absence from the scene had been a blessing.

CIV.

There is no courage in the headlong rush
　　Upon the foe, when every pulse is stirr'd.
Action the coward will a moment flush
　　Into a hero, when the trumpets' heard,
And charging squadrons emulously push
　　Forward, careering madly at the word—
This needs no courage.　When the blood is heated
Will fight the veriest lamb that ever bleated.

CV.

" But to stand calmly while the bullets whiz
　　Around you, popping off, at times, a friend,
And passing close to your own proper phiz,
　　Making you think of your approaching end.
This—this true brav'ry past all doubting is
　　As every soldier well may comprehend—
Death stares you in the face—there's no escaping—
Your very grave is to your fancy gaping.

CVI.

" There was a young lieutenant in the prime
　　Of manhood's early bloom—behind me trying
'To keep the soldiers steady—at a time
　　When some could hardly be restrain'd from flying—
While others, fiery as that eastern clime,
　　Boil'd with impatience to behold the dying
And dead fall unaveng'd, without attempting
A forward rush, from fate themselves exempting.

CVII.

" His voice was heard above all others, cheering
　　The men, and bidding them preserve their line,
Assuring them the gun the fort was nearing,
　　And they would soon effect each have design ;
He knew their mettle, but their rashness fearing,
　　He bade them not at the command repine—
As to the shrinkers, death without delaying,
He threatened to those cowardice displaying.

CVIII.

" He had but join'd us a few weeks before,
    Leaving a young and very lovely bride.
Himself he had distinguish'd at Cawnpore
    When he and I combated side by side.
At morn when me reclining he bent o'er,
    Around his neck I saw a portrait tied;
Which he kiss'd lovingly, me quite forgetting,
As to our troop we early out were setting.

CIX.

" One to the other we had ta'en a liking—
    I was a sprightly fellow in my youth,
But altogether not in form so striking,
    As was my gallant friend, Lieutenant Routh—
For thirty years I've carried arms for my King,
    Nor e'er a better soldier knew in sooth;
And our acquaintance into friendship warm'd
Had been by gallant deeds by each perform'd.

CX.

" He was no officer who follow'd fashion,
    No dandy got up by an army tailor—
Glory with him was a consuming passion,
    And in hot fight he never was a quailer.
The foe to him 'twas happiness to dash on,
    Who found he was a terrible assailer.
Had he but liv'd, to me it seems quite clear,
Posterity had nam'd him with Napier.

CXI.

" But fate ordain'd it otherwise.   He fell—
    A bullet struck him just above the eye.
Upward he sprang convulsive—as I tell
    The story now I can't restrain a sigh."
The Major's quiv'ring voice here ceas'd to dwell
    Upon his tale.   His wine-glass to supply
He grasp'd the bottle—Sorrow overcame him.
For such a feeling none could surely blame him.

CXII.

" Upward he sprang—then, stretch'd upon the ground,
     With life extinct, his rigid body lay,"
Resum'd our host—" When in our rear the sound
     Of the appaoaching gun forbad delay—
Or in his bosom I had doubtless found
     The miniature and carried it away.
His mourning widow, from it, consolation
Might have receiv'd in her life's desolation.

CXIII.

" But time there was not for the slightest pause—
     The piece of ordnance now had gain'd the hill,
And soon upon the gate its blacken'd jaws
     Shot after shot, belch'd forth, incessant till
Of our first check in fragments sank the cause,
     When, with a rush, we did the entrance fill.
Beyond it was a passage—where a stand
Still the foe made, fighting us hand to hand.

CXIV.

" I tell you seriously it was no joke,
     That close encounter with the natives there.
Now a sword cut, now from a spear a poke
     (While musket-balls by hundreds fill'd the air),
Made it unpleasant.   Aim'd a sabre stroke
     At me a savage, furious with despair—
Exerting my full strength the blow I parried,
And well it was for me that it miscarried.

CXV.

" To clear the passage we contriv'd, altho'
     'Twas intricate, with many a bend and turn ;
Which made our slaughtering progress rather slow,
     Each inch of ground being won by combat stern.
McLeod was not the man to shun a foe,
     But look'd on peril with much unconcern.
As when his sires wielded the claymore
Along his path there ran a stream of gore.

CXVI.

" We struggled o'er the dying and the dead,
    To find another gate impede our course—
Within it, some, on our advance, had fled ;
    The greater part, indeed, to this resource
Betook themselves, when they perceiv'd the head,
    The first gate thro', of our advancing force.
The rest, a small determin'd body, died
Beneath our bay'nets, fighting side by side.

CXVII.

" Again we were compell'd to use the gun
    Which burst the gate with a tremendous crash
In a short time ; and thro' the portal won,
    We pass'd, victorious by that levelling smash—
No one oppos'd us here—our work was done,
    We thought—but undeceiv'd were by the flash
Of musketry once more—a storm of shot
Pour'd again on us deadly at this spot.

CXVIII.

" Another passage, like the former, seem'd
    To lead to the interior—the walls
Being pierc'd with loopholes, out of which there gleam'd
    Full many a musket ; and within the calls
Of shouting men and women, too, that scream'd,
    Our ears saluted, 'mid a shower of balls.
There was of wounds and falling men no dearth,
And here if anywhere was hell on earth.

CXIX.

" The passage terminated in a gate—
    To Hercules, when he the Hydra slew,
As one head perish'd 'neath the pond'rous weight
    Of his descending club, another grew—
So, as each portal fell by efforts great,   ·
    Another rose to our desponding view ;
Again our cannon to remove it thunder'd,
While we, how many more would check us, wonder'd.

CXX.

" This obstacle but faint resistance made,
  The wood in splinters flew, as it was batter'd,
And we could see the natives shrink dismay'd
    As balls and fragments in their midst were scatter'd ;
For our men us'd their muskets, when display'd
    Were the defenders thro' the portal shatter'd—
They fled, as we advanc'd, to clear the gateway—
To the main keep, not distant now a great way.

CXXI.

" We pushed along the passage till we reach'd,
  Another gate, the fourth, which to us offer'd
Again a barrier, also to be breach'd
    By our artillery whose aid was proffer'd
And us'd in vain —the gunners' skill impeach'd
    Our leader ; and the soldiers were to scoff heard
At their balk'd comrades.   Truly our position
Somewhat excus'd the angry ebullition.

CXXII.

" We were in what the Yankee's call a 'fix :'
  The enemy were firing from within—
And every passing moment five or six
    Of our fellows lost the power to sin —
We could but burst the gate or ' cut our sticks,'
    Which latter course we thought of with chagrin.
Some how or other when one's been retreating
Men think one has been forc'd back by a beating.

CXXIII.

" McLeod here luckily observ'd a wicket,
  Against which now our cannon was directed,
And burst it open—merry as a cricket,
    Ere on the accident the foe reflected,
Like a late passenger to obtain his ticket
    When the train's smoke approaching is detected—
Rush'd in the Major, and we follow'd quickly,
Cutting those down who pressed upon us thickly.

CXXIV.

" This is the last event I can remember,
　　Save a bright flash which made my optics quail,
And then a blow, that shook my every member,
　　Flooring me like weak saplings does a gale;
Extinguish'd then I deem'd the vital ember—
　　In sooth my hold on life was very frail.
The men imagin'd I had my quietus,
And fear'd when I fell that the foe would beat us.

CXXV.

" 'Twas sev'ral days ere from my swoon I woke,
　　When I was told the fortress had been gain'd.
By this achievement we completely broke,
　　In that vicinity, what still remain'd
Of native power, and beneath the yoke
　　To pass of Britain were our foes constrain'd,
For Alighur had been their main depôt—
How it was lost and won I've let you know."

CXXVI.

The Major stopp'd and lighted his cigar,
　　Gave a long whiff, then look'd for our applause;
He was delighted with his deeds of war,
　　And thought them of the victory a cause—
But this his history did little mar.
　　Of modesty he well preserv'd the laws.
His heroes were McLeod and his friend Routh;
And so he did not go beyond the truth.

CXXVII.

The look he gave us when the tale was finish'd,
　　However, very plainly intimated
The chance of vict'ry 'd not have been diminish'd,
　　Had he to lead at Alighur been fated.
We told him, as his wine-glass he replenish'd,
　　We much admir'd his story animated,
Thanking him for the spirited narration
Which had supplied our lack of conversation.

H

CXXVIII.

Just then the sable Major-domo shew'd
  His curly pate within the opening door.
"Tea ready, massa," was its owner's mode
  Of hinting, for us was prepar'd to pour
The washy beverage by the cast bestow'd,
  The lady of the house presiding o'er
Her "equipage," behind a steaming urn,
Anxious that we the wine had left to learn.

CXXIX.

"Another glass," the jovial vet'ran cried,
  "And ere we join 'em, let us toast the 'ladies.'
To them we owe, it cannot be denied,
  The greatest pleasure which to each convey'd is.
Drink then to those we love—him woe betide
  By whom excuse to fill a bumper made is;
Hip, hip hurrah—let's have the Kentish fire,
Thinking, the while, on those whom we admire."

CXXX.

We fill'd our glasses; and impetuous rose
  In prompt approval of the Major's toast.
Duncan of Bella thought, as I suppose,
  And of his vocal powers made the most;
I bawl'd out, too, my wine beneath my nose,
  In imitation of my friend, and host—
Of whom I thought I need not here explain,
Those who don't know have read my verse in vain.

CXXXI.

This is the end of Canto Fourth;—I'm thinking
  'Tis an improvement upon Canto Third.
Bright was the thought to leave my heroes drinking,
  For that they happy were, must be inferr'd,
When so employ'd. If o'er my page not winking,
  Nor deeming my rhymes doggrel and absurd,
Turn it, my gentle reader, and proceed
With Canto Fifth, which now awaits your heed.

END OF CANTO IV.

CANTO V.

—

I.

It seems to me a curious speculation,
     How ancient ladies did contrive to utter
Their various scandals, holding conversation,
     Before was added *tea* to bread and butter.
Imagine now the dreadful consternation
     Which coteries would put into a flutter
If the Celestials should cease to sell us
The leaf, in which producing, they excel us.

II.

In days of old we read of " Good Queen Bess
     Slaking her morning thirst with potent beer."
Did this of female elocution less
     Inspire than the infusion with which cheer,
Themselves old maids and wives, when they confess
     Langour with their good health to interfere ;
Or must we be compell'd to understand all
Were introduc'd at once, both Tea and Scandal ?

III.

Then in the reign of our Charles the Second,
     We hear of Tea as a rare commodity—
That epoch truly *scandalous* is reckon'd !
     Tho' a *Tea*-drinker then was quite an oddity—
And grocers at their doors a neighbour beckon'd,
     As his white apron each did round his body tie,
To shew him the new sign, where Innovation
Strange drinks was selling to a wond'ring nation.

IV.

Old Peppys with gusto talks of having taken
    A cup of *Tea*, as of a new liqueur.
Perhaps that very cup in him did waken—
    Which makes his copious pen so often err,
The love of scandal.   Had he not forsaken
    Wine and strong beer—much is it to aver
Less of detraction had contain'd his Diary?
The question's dubious, and demands enquiry.

V.

With what disgust, on looking at the past,
    Must your teetotaler regard his sires?
Had Tea upon our shores been never cast,
    What would have been his "drink" to quench the fire
Of thirst?—for as a stimulant is class'd
    The leaf with which he pampers his desires,
In my opinion—spite of all his faction ;
And on the nerves injurious is its action.

VI.

Now, in our shops there is no lack of tea,
    Neither, alas! of scandal at our tables.
The small-talk there is altogether free,
    Turning too often on the wildest fables,
In which are mention'd one, or two, or three,
    Dwelling the nearest to each mentor's gables.
Did they drink wine, or beer, or even water,
Perhaps our dames would give their friends some quarter.

VII.

But to resume.   Reluctantly our host
    The table left—we follow'd his example—
He seem'd unwilling to desert his post,
    Though his potations had indeed, been ample—
But Bill and I desir'd tea and toast,
    And he could not upon our wishes trample.
He rose—his movement slightly was unsteady—
Saying "to join the ladies he was ready."

VIII.

Seated we found the twain, in expectation
    Of our arrival; and with much parade,
Coupling the action with a dissertation,
    Handed Mamma to each the tea she'd made;
Beside her was again my situation,
    At which I felt, I must confess, dismay'd.
The Major while of tea she spoke, the joys on,
Sipp'd his—like Socrates imbibing poison.

IX.

He sat beside me.—On the other side
    The loving pair—within themselves a world—
Heedless that Father Time did past them glide,
    Talk'd in low tone—where Bella's ringlets curl'd
And glossy, with the worm's web silken vied,
    Bill bent his head—while with his hand he twirl'd
The massive gold chain that secur'd her watch.
I saw the father knew it was a match.

X.

He guess'd I felt distaste for my position,
    And mov'd uneasily upon his chair,
Seeming to signify he felt contrition
    For having suffer'd me to settle there
Close to his wife, and pitied my condition,
    Altho' his feelings he would not declare;
And after tea was finish'd me invited
To walk out with him—I complied, delighted.

XI.

We took our hats and stepp'd into the garden—
    'Tis true, I did not much admire my man,
But one who travels, never should be hard on
    The foibles which make others form a plan
Of action differing from his own—I pardon
    All such as fully as a mortal can—
Besides so tiresome was the lady's chatter,
I thought the Major's might improve the matter.

XII.

The moon shone brightly as we issued forth,
    And 'mongst the shrubs and flow'rs, the night breeze play'd,
Not coldly blowing from the boist'rous north,
    But gently from the south, as if afraid
To injure, in its course, some bud of worth,
    Unnotic'd yet, and modest as a maid—
Plenty of "Moon" I have already giv'n,
To poets it would seem the whole of Heav'n.

XIII.

And yet on moonless nights, I've gazing been,
    At the stars scatter'd o'er the azure sky—
I could not name each twinkler on the scene,
    But the grand whole no less entranc'd my eye—
All objects bath'd too in the silvery sheen,
    On earth, in picturesque repose did lie.
Why should the moon alone usurp all praise,
While the sweet stars emit their softer rays?

XIV.

I know not. But to me it e'er has chanc'd,
    Having receiv'd of poems a collection,
When towards the index I my eye have glanc'd,
    To find a sonnet, meeting my inspection,
To the moon there; and, in the book, advanc'd,
    I always dwelt upon an interjection
As its commencement—generally " oh !"
'Tis p'rhaps correct the moon to speak to so.

XV.

Not to the moon—but to my host I talk'd—
    Who was a planet of another sphere,
As in the garden eisurely we walk'd—
    His voice contrasting as it reach'd my ear,
With the brook's murmur, where its stream was balk'd
    Or nearly, as it tried a course to clear
Amongst the stones—and the low night breeze sighing
So gently, we might deem that *sound* was dying.

XVI.

I need not tell you that our conversation
    Cigars accompanied.   A constant smoker
Was the old soldier, and to fumigation
    [of tobacco was a great provoker;
It soothed the Major's mental irritation,
    When he could march as stiff as any poker,
Cooling his temper with the weed Virginian,
Himself *subliming* in his own opinion.

XVII.

So half an hour pleasantly we spent,
    When my companion suddenly suggested
It was high time to join the men we went,
    If to mix with them I felt interested.
" On doing so," I answered, " I am bent,
    For with such mystery appears invested
Your groom—I long to hear him make a speech,
To do which I've been told him ' grog' can teach."

XVIII.

So forthwith to the kitchen we proceeded,
    Where round the stove we found the mowers sitting,
And with them, Adam, who, in silence heeded
    What there occurr'd—the " darkey's" restless flitting,
As if repose his body never needed,
    His lady anything but fair—in knitting
Busied—ourselves, arriv'd to join the party,
Whose welcome of us vulgar was, but hearty.

XIX.

The Major took a snug seat in the corner,
    And not far from him I procur'd a chair—
He sent the Nigger in to Mrs. Horner,
    To fetch some whiskey, that we might not share
The men's, which was Canadian—for a scorner
    Of that he loudly did himself declare;
It was too raw and fiery for his drinking.
In the same way, I also, was of thinking.

XX.

The rest imbib'd the native spirit gaily,
　　Till their eyes sparkled with imparted fire—
The canny Scotchman warming did not fail high
　　Truths to inculcate, and to name his sire
And all his clan, which in his mouth were daily,
　　And Paddy talk'd of Erin's wrongs with ire ;
While the third man, a genuine John Bull,
Kept his tongue silent and his noggin full.

XXI.

Old Adam now and then put in a word,
　　But still his silence was not wholly thaw'd ;
'Twas at long intervals his voice was heard,
　　As he his horn affectionately paw'd.
To me and to the Major he referred
　　For an opinion, by our presence aw'd—
When any matter of dispute arose,
That our decision might prevent hard blows.

XXII.

Our gallant host sat solemnly in state,
　　Like the presiding judge at a court-martial ;
Save that his toddy he drank at a rate,
　　Which shew'd him to the composition partial,
And said when finish'd was a hot debate,
　　" All from disputing henceforth I debar shall.
Adam will give us briefly the narration,
Of what decided him on emigration.

XXIII.

" Or p'rhaps, as I observe, he's in the vein—
　　He'll tell, at length, the story of his life.
The retrospection will not give him pain,
　　Howe'er it may with trouble have been rife.
For age of sorrows past does not complain
　　Like fiery youth impatient with the strife
Of worldly contests.　This myself I feel,
Tho' than him younger to whom I appeal.

XXIV.

" Come then my friend (to Adam, turning), speak.
    For your commencement anxiously we're listening—
Tell us of fortune by what curious freak,
    Over your whiskey here your eyes are glistening.
I know no more your tale than I do Greek,
    So you begin must with your birth and christening."
The Major ceas'd, and took a sip of toddy,
Then in his chair he settled his small body.

XXV.

" *Conticuere omnes*," says the bard,
    Whose verse describes the sorrows of Queen Dido,
When to narrate his tale and fortune hard
    He makes his hero just the same as I do
Mine of this Canto. I have small regard,
    For Kings and " Royal right divine" deny do.
And so no prince, but simple Adam Faber,
I've made my hero, who was born to labour.

XXVI.

But while I'm on the subject, let me say
    Why Virgil " Pious" calls Anchises' son
I never understood. The Roman way
    Of thinking of " sweet woman" when undone,
And her undoer will suit many a gay
    Lothario, of which class I'm not one;
But would not now-a-days be thought quite moral,
So on this point I with the Mantuan quarrel.

XXVII.

Besides, I think the Trojan was an ass,
    Carthage being ready built for him to rule,
O'er such an opportunity to pass;
    And with the obstinacy of a mule,
Instead of marrying the royal lass,
    The whining scamp! about his fate to pule
And sail away—his mistress sad deceiving,
Not even telling her that he was leaving.

XXVIII.

This in a Roman's eye might seem like "piety."
    Rascality, I call it—also folly;
When the Phœnician's charms had brought satiety,
    The pious man of course grew melancholy—
The veil was rais'd which love's first inebriety,
    With magic skill had cast upon his "Dolly"—
So he levanted, going upon a cruise,
To seek more girls to love—more men to bruise.

XXIX.

Such piety as this these latter days
    Have not produced—but something quite as bad—
'Tis "impious," from the ground your eyes to raise,
    More "impious" still, to look a moment glad.
Long pray'rs and speeches,—abstinence from plays,
    And balls, and cards, and missionaries mad
Supported by subscribers madder—these
Form now "the piety" the saints to please.

XXX.

The cholera's among us here again—
    The saints are anxious to proclaim a fast.*
To Palmerston they've written in this vein,
    A letter, which, I think will be their last.
Of his impiety they will complain,
    Because as zanies he's politely class'd.
Men, who, instead of filth removing, pray,
Thinking the stench will thus be drain'd away.

XXXI.

Conticuere omnes, as the man,
    Remarkable for silence, thus his tale
In a low faltering voice to tell began.
    "I'm old; and my dim eyes already fail,
And the legs totter with which erst I ran,
    And aches and pains do now my frame assail—
Tho' I was once as sturdy as the oak,
Ere on my youth the storm of trouble broke.

---

* This is an allusion to certain Saints in Edinburgh, who remonstrated with Lord Palmerston, when Home Secretary, because he had not advised the Queen to proclaim a Fast in 1853, when the Cholera was raging in the **metropolis** of Scotland.

XXXII.

" But, as the Major says, I must commence
　　E'en from the opening of my humble life,
When first I found the use of every sense,
　　Not dreaming that with ill the world was rife.
I will unbosom—using no pretence
　　Aught to conceal,—I never had a wife,
And so to no one have I hitherto
Told the sad tale I'm telling now to you.

XXXIII.

" My father was a labourer, and dwelt
　　At a small hamlet, near a country town
In Oxfordshire; my other parent dealt
　　In tapes, and small-wares, tramping up and down,
Whether the sunshine or the rain she felt,
　　The hilly district, meeting smile or frown
With the same calm endurance.　Could she sell
A trifling article, it paid her well.

XXXIV.

" While she was absent, driving thus her trade,
　　I to a neighbour's wife was given in charge,
To whom a trivial recompense was made,
　　Which somewhat did her scanty means enlarge.
Our whitewashed cottage stood beneath the shade
　　Of an old oak—a public-house, ' the Barge,'
Join'd it.　In front there was the village-green,
And opposite, my nurse's house was seen.

XXXV.

" Her daughter was a pretty little girl,
　　Ruddy and fat, with sweet blue sparkling eyes,
And flaxen ringlets that did flowing curl.
　　She was my playmate.—On my mem'ry rise
The sunny mornings, when I'd sit and twirl
　　Her glossy hair—both gazing at the skies,
Then on the green before us, to each sound
Intently listening, which rose around.

XXXVI.

" This is my first remembrance.   Then, a boy,
  In her short journeys, by my mother's side,
Before the farmers me could find employ,
  Aping the man, I did ambitious stride.
The village school-dame work'd me much annoy,
  Striving in learning's path my mind to guide ;
But from her often-times I play'd the truant,
So doing to example bad pursuant.

XXXVII.

" However, she contriv'd to make me learn
  To read my Bible, and a little writing,
So that I was enabled to discern
  The right way from the wrong—altho' inviting
Oft is the latter, making mortals yearn
  For pleasures just a moment, them delighting—
But, which are follow'd by whole years of pain,
So that we lose when most we seem to gain.

XXXVIII.

" Pleasure is like a bee upon the wing,
  With honey gather'd from a fragrant flow'r
Laden, sweet increase to her hive to bring,
  Collected during many a weary hour.
Man is a child, who, heedless of the sting,
  Wishing the luscious load were in his pow'r,
The insect grasps—his booty he has won,
But the smart tells him he has badly done.

XXXIX.

" Alice, my baby play-mate, was at school
  The constant solace of my boyish woes.
We occupied, when learning. the same stool,
  And with each other frolicked when we rose.
My faults she told me when I play'd the fool,
  And hated heartily my youthful foes.
To learn she coax'd me, I could not resist her.
I always call'd her my sweet little sister.

XL.

" The days allow'd the poor at school are few.
  The struggle for subsistence calls away
The boy, before he gains the sense to rue
  The time he's squander'd in excessive play.
When I was bigger grown a horn I blew,
  Wond'ring each hour, how long would last the day
In fields where seed-corn had been lately sown,
Which the rooks coveted to make their own.

XLI.

" But still to school I went when occupation
  Was in no other way for me provided ;
And so I got the little education
  I have,—a blessing not to be derided—
For, if to me, it have not prov'd salvation,
  From many evils which my fate supply did.
At least it taught me somewhat to endure 'em,
Softening their pangs, altho' it could not cure 'em.

XLII.

" In harvest time we were allow'd to glean
  (The women and the children of the village),
When carried safely to the yard had been
  The shocks of corn, so that we could not pillage.
This practice is invariably seen
  In England, 'mongst the folks engaged in tillage.
It adds a trifle to the labourer's store,
Keeping the gaunt wolf famine from the door.

XLIII.

" To drive the horses while the teamster plough'd,
  With Farmer Brown, I next obtain'd employment ;
I recollect, at first, I felt quite proud,
  And the work was a positive enjoyment.
I thought to me a boon had been allow'd,
  Which, that I was no longer deem'd a boy, meant,
But soon my aching legs, when day expir'd,
Upon me brought conviction, I was tir'd.

XLIV.

" In short, away my boyish days so glided,
    That when I had attain'd my sixteenth year,
My little term of life to me divided,
    'Twixt work and play, and learning did appear ;
Joyous, and tall, and hearty, I derided
    Of future trouble anything like fear.
I little knew how soon it would o'ertake me,
And how forlorn and wretched it would make me.

XLV.

" Alice was now a lovely girl become.
    Her bright blue eyes shone with more thrilling fire.
Her mother kept her constantly at home,
    And all my evenings I spent sitting by her,
It seem'd so natural.—Hints already, some,
    I, for a wife, my playmate did desire,
Began to give me, at which I felt flatter'd.
Alas ! such hopes were soon, for ever shatter'd.

XLVI.

" Stourton, the hamlet where we liv'd, was plac'd
    Upon a hill.—Below there was a vale ;
In which my young eye oft with pleasure trac'd
    The brook, now flashing broad in the mill tail ;
Now in a sweep confin'd, which willows grac'd,
    Gliding conceal'd, so that my gaze would fail
To catch its stream reflecting the sun's ray,
Where in deep pools the pike pursued their prey.

XLVII.

" Thro' meadows it meander'd—Here a bend.
    Encroach'd on the intensely verdant plain—
There its straight course some distance did extend,
    Till the eye sought its silvery line in vain.
Trees in the hedge-rows, up the slope did blend
    With pastures and enclosures bright with grain,
To form a landscape, with such beauty teeming,
One almost thought the sight of it was dreaming.

XLVIII.

" Across the brook, down to its very brink,
    Planted with ancient oaks and ashes tall,
Whose boughs the waters anxious seemed to drink,
    A park expanded, rising to the hall ;
Which amongst shrubb'ries did coyly shrink,
    So that a glimpse you caught but of its wall,
By time discolor'd thro' the foilage peeping,
And of the church which holds its founder sleeping.

XLIX.

" The Squire, the owner of the place I mention,
    Was an old gentleman of near threescore—
He did not think it any condescension,
    Nor unbefitting of the name he bore,
To his inferiors to give attention,
    Who for his aid or counsel did implore.
To all his tenants he was kind and affable,
Admiring everything jocose and laughable.

L.

" He was a fine old man.   His ruddy face
    Broad and good-humour'd, wore a constant smile ;
Of grief, or care, or pride, there was no trace—
    Nor of bad passions, nor of lurking guile
In its expression.   True, devoid of grace
    Was his stout form, cloth'd in the olden style—
But still 'twas evident by Nature's plan,
He was intended for a ' gentleman.'

LI.

" He farm'd some portion of his own estate,
    Preserv'd his game too strictly, I confess.
Poachers to him were vermin ; whom to hate
    Seem'd natural.   He therefore laid more stress
On an offence which tended to abate
    His stock of birds than anyone would guess—
A pack of hounds he kept and hunters many,
Which he himself could ride as well as any.

LII.

" His hospitality being known to all,
        Became proverbial on ev'ry tongue.
The honest laborer did never call
        At the old house but he its praises sung ;
For to his portion there were sure to fall
        Some beer and food the serving-men among—
In fine, there was no gentleman whose bounty
Could be compar'd to his throughout the county.

LIII.

" I've often seen him in his scarlet coat,
        On winter mornings going to meet his hounds ;
Riding a horse, whose beauty did denote,
        He'd cost his jovial master many pounds.
' What riches does that happy man devote,'
        Was my reflection, ' to his spacious grounds,
His gamekeepers, preserves, and grooms, and horses.
Would make us poor folks wealthy, his resources.'

LIV.

" His name was Strathern.   I was just sixteen,
        When I was hired as a stable lad
By his stud-groom, who long had friendly been
        With both my parents ; and was therefore glad
With his good offices to intervene,
        To place me where I should be fed and clad
With comfort from my wage.   Thus was I made
A groom ; and grooming since has been my trade.

LV.

" This was indeed a lift in life for me.
        My father thought my humble fortune made—
And to the Hall I took my way with glee,
        Tho' as I gain'd the lodge I felt afraid—
Strange faces I had never lov'd to see,
        Even of those belonging to my grade,
And the smart servants fill'd my mind with dread.
They seem'd to me so *fine,* and so *high*-bred.

LVI.

"I had seen Alice just before I started,
    And taken leave of her with many a sigh—
Her lips I kiss'd with fervor ere we parted,
    Tho' from the contact she essay'd to fly
In vain.   But from my arms in haste she darted,
    Shock'd at my inroad on her modesty,
As soon as I, too good to be neglected,
Deeming the chance, my purpose had effected

LVII.

"I thought of her sweet blushing little face,
    As up the stately avenue I strode,
Lingering the way along with listless pace,
    While apprehension did my spirits load
Of those I must consort with at the place
    Where I was going to take up my abode.
At last my stock of confidence I muster'd,
Reaching the court-yard, not a little fluster'd.

LVIII.

"I found my friend, the stud-groom, in the stable,
    Where with the horses sev'ral lads and men,
Industrious, apparently as able,
    Were working cheerfully beneath his ken—
Produc'd their varied hissing, quite a Babel
    Of sounds I never heard so loud as then,
Which jarr'd upon my ear—with great delight
He seem'd to listen—thinking 'twas all right.

LIX.

"I waited with him till each horse was fed,
    And litter'd comfortably down with straw,
So that he might repose him on his bed;
    And his especial fav'rites with his paw
Patted my friend; then from the stable led
    The way in search of food for his own maw—
Follow'd the rest, and he turn'd in the lock
The key as it was striking eight o'clock.

LX.

" 'Twas Autumn—nigh upon the hunting season ;
    So that much work there was in exercising
And doing other things each groom agrees on,
    As fit at both sunset and eke sun-rising,
(To gainsay which 'mongst hunters would be treason)
    To bring with art as tedious as surprising,
His master's horses into good condition,
Which is the topmost height of his ambition.

LXI.

" We gain'd the house, and soon our suppers smok'd
    Upon the table—bread and beef and beer—
The stable-lads and men all blithesome jok'd,
    As they prepar'd them for their evening cheer—
Lonesome I felt among them, but I cloak'd
    My feelings, trying joyous to appear.
In a back kitchen 'twas we took our meal,
Two scullery girls attending us with zeal.

LXII.

" The upper servants and my friend, the groom,
    Consorted with each other in the hall—
A lofty spacious and commodious room,
    Where was admitted no inferior thrall.
The ladies' maids did there in finery bloom,
    Whom our soil'd hands and jerkins did appal—
And girls all hot and steaming from the scullery,
With such smart madams did not fail to pull awry.

LXIII.

· " In all society there is gradation,
    Tho' Yankees here preach much of their equality,
And, in accordance with my observation,
    Even where rules supreme their boasted polity—
The man of wealth is more in estimation
    Than he who cant afford t' indulge in jollity—
It seems to me a scheme by Nature plann'd,
That some should serve—some have the upper hand.

LXIV.

" However, at the hall an aristocracy,
    And of the haughtiest in its mood prevail'd,
Looking upon us lads as a democracy,
    By whom their order p'rhaps might be assail'd.
The Squire of course rul'd all by an autocracy,
    Save what his wife's and valet's will avail'd.
The latter thought himself a man superior,
Hinting to him his master was inferior.

LXV.

" The steward and the housekeeper apart
    Liv'd from the rest, and with them the man-cook;
When he had ceas'd from practising his art,
    Which of the day but very little took.
He mostly slept when idle, and would start
    At times, and gaze with a bewilder'd look.
That he was French his language did betoken,
Being partly native,—partly English broken.

LXVI.

" All this from my associates I glean'd,
    Who those they envied, scandaliz'd of course;
The absent from detraction are not screen'd
    By merit, which sometimes provokes its force,
But as with haughtiness themselves demean'd,
    The parties who supplied us with discourse,
That disposition did in nowise tend
To soften ranc'rous talk, you may depend.

LXVII.

" Early we all retir'd for the night,
    And when I reach'd my chamber I became
With my position overpower'd quite,
    So that to rest I could not soothe my frame.
The loneliness I felt, was like a blight
    Upon my young heart—I have had the same
Sensations since—but with less of intensity;
For to such, years decreases the propensity.

LXVIII.

"I thought of my home, which tho' humble, shone
    Now I had left it, with a thousand charms,
Of what for me my parents' kind had done,
        While I liv'd there—of Alice in my arms,
When I that kiss so stealthily had won,
        In spite of all her modesty's alarms.
At length these memories faded into slumber,
When dreams oppres'd me more than I can number.

LXIX.

"I rose refresh'd, howe'er, at morning's prime,
    And had my work alloted like the rest.
Custom and youth, and health, combin'd with time,
        Lighten'd the sadness which had me oppress'd.
In joking, I could with my fellows chime
        As blithely, on occasion, as the best.
Also I learnt to groom a horse and ride him,
And over hedge and ditch to boldly guide him.

LXX.

"Twelve months and more of life thus passed away.
    I went to see my parents ev'ry week,
And Alice with whom ling'ring I could stay
        Till night advancing bade me Strathern seek.
Most anxious were my longings for the day,
        When we th' irrevocable words should speak ;
More womanly and lovelier she had grown,
And me had promis'd to become my own.

LXXI.

"But we were young—her mother bade us wait.
    Waiting, alas ! affects a lover's heart
With doubts and sad presentiments—a state
        Of mind producing—like the constant smart
Of a deep wound, when pain nought can abate,
        Whatever anodynes skill may impart.
Ah ! Love, with hope deferr'd, is most unpleasant,
For to the soul it torments brings incessant.

LXXII.

" About this time the squire's son return'd
     From College, where he'd studied ancient lore.
What from his books and tutors he had learn'd
     I had not car'd—had he known nothing more.
But in his handsome face I soon discern'd
     Desires he'd never gain'd from books of yore—
His form was finely moulded—so that all
The ladies'-maids in love with him did fall.

LXXIII.

" He was his mother's pride; an only son,
     An only child—the last of his long line,
Which had in ages past bright honour won,
     Whose virtues were in him again to shine.
This was her fervent wish—She dwelt upon
     Its consummation as the sole design
Of her existence; and she fondly deem'd
Her boy was all her doating heart had dream'd.

LXXIV.

" True, he was handsome—aye, so *beautiful*
     In face and figure, one might well believe
A Son of Heaven had come down to cull
     Earth's loveliest flow'r.—Such did erst receive
Men's blooming daughters—when mankind as dull
     And base, for seraph-lovers they would leave—
The Bible tells us this; and woman still
By the same feeling is betrayed to ill.

LXXV.

" And he was clever—had those winning ways
     Which steal insensibly upon the heart;
He knew how woman's ear delights in praise,
     And where to aim deception's honied dart!
Himself all smiles, responding smiles could raise,
     Or cause with pathos pitying tears to start;
In female conquests 'twas his pride to revel,
His outside heav'nly—but within a Devil.

LXXVI.

" He was my senior—but twenty years
　　Of life as yet he scarcely had beheld.
His past career his father fill'd with fears,
　　Which from his wife he studiously withheld;
The wildest rake among his young compeers,
　　From college he had nearly been expell'd—
Escaping narrowly with rustication,
Which, it was thought, *might* work his reformation.

LXXVII.

" His banishment he came to spend at home.
　　His mother welcom'd him; his father frown'd;
He wish'd, himself, in foreign lands to roam,
　　But with his sire some difficulty found,
Who thought attachment to each classic tome
　　Better for him than quitting English ground—
And so of studying pretence he made,
With very little progress, I'm afraid.

LXXVIII.

" He treated all the servants with contempt.
　　Even the valet was not an exception,
Who did familiarity attempt,
　　But met with anything but the reception
He'd calculated on; and quite exempt
　　Was the young squire's manner from deception.
He told the man he would not brook intrusion,
So that the flunkey left him in confusion.

LXXIX.

" I was at first a favourite, and long
　　Regarded him with ev'ry friendly feeling,
Me he selected from the grooms among,
　　To ride with him at times; and so appealing
To my young vanity, he gain'd a strong
　　Hold on my heart; with slight advances stealing
Into my breast—till I began to love him,
And wonder'd why his father should reprove him.

LXXX.

"It chanc'd one day, after a glorious run,
  In which we foremost rode—our horses tir'd—
Homeward as we return'd at setting sun,
  Thro' Stourton, she, whom I so much admir'd,
Ran to her mother's door elate with fun,
  Thinking that I to speak to her desir'd;
But when she saw my master back she drew,
Her young face colouring with a crimson hue.

LXXXI.

"I saw young Strathern glance with his bright eye
  At the fair object of my youthful love;
And as she spoke, and I made short reply,
  Biting, he sat uneasily, his glove—
I thought, too, he repressed a rising sigh,
  As o'er her form his gaze did prying rove.
But he ask'd merely as we rode away,
If she, my sister were, who bade me stay.

LXXXII.

"I answer'd 'No!' No other words were us'd,
  But moodily tow'rds Strathern we rode on,
The youthful 'squire evidently mus'd
  On the sweet creature which my heart had won—
My wayward fate I afterwards accus'd
  For this sad chance, and curs'd my father's son;
That I myself had been the cause which led,
To all the misery doom'd for my poor head.

LXXXIII.

"As time elaps'd, still kinder Edward grew
  (For so the 'squire's only son was nam'd),
And closer in attendance on him drew
  Myself, whose services he always claim'd.
When he and Alice met, I never knew,
  First, after this. I saw she felt asham'd
When of my master I made casual mention,
To find the cause of which tax'd my invention.

LXXXIV.

" The winter pass'd away.   Fair spring awoke
    With all its budding leaves and opening flow'rs.
Then imperceptibly upon us broke
    Summer, and with it bright and sunny hours ;
Summer—which gladness should from all evoke,
    Which stirs the heart with its enlivening pow'rs—
When I, alas! observ'd in Alice coldness,
For now she chid me oft-times for my boldness.

LXXXV.

" But still I could not well divine the cause.
    I'd never seen her with my master's heir.
I felt suspicious, but compell'd to pause
    Before I should my doubts to her declare—
We all know jealousy its trust withdraws,
    Stung to the quick by ' trifles light as air.'
Against this feeling I was on my guard,
Till I discover'd all my hopes were marr'd.

LXXXVI.

" It was a lovely evening in July.
    After a sultry day, a cooling breeze
Rose, ere the sun sank down in majesty,
    And gently stirr'd the foliage of the trees.
It was not dark as yet, when forward I
    Set (for to send me did my mistress please
Then on an errand) to a place not distant,
To do some work she needed an assistant.

LXXXVII.

" The footpath along which I took my way,
    Led o'er the meadows and across the brook
(Where it our custom long had been to stray,
    Myself and Alice) to a shelter'd nook,
Where grew an aged oak, whose stem's decay
    A hollow and fantastic figure took.
Within this hollow we had often sat,
Whiling the hours away in loving chat.

LXXXVIII.

" The opening look'd upon the murmuring stream,
     And clustering ivy cover'd all the trunk,
Save where the entrance was ; and you might deem
     It a lone cell for cremite or monk,
His solitary life away to dream,
     Into abstraction melancholy sunk ;
And as you cross'd the bridge your eye might gain
A glimpse of those the hollow did contain.

LXXXIX.

" This point I reach'd, when fell upon my ear
     The sound of smother'd voices ; and I stopp'd.
The evening was so mild, serene, and clear,
     I caught each syllable the couple dropp'd ;
For there were two within the tree so near
     To the foot-path.   Beneath a willow lopp'd
I took my station—listening until
The voices ceas'd, and all around was still.

XC.

" One voice was that of Alice ; and my name
     Was mention'd by her, not in terms of praise.
I felt a tremor running thro' my frame,
     As, towards the tree, was riveted my gaze.
Who was her partner there in sin and shame ?
     The truth upon my jealous heart did blaze—
It must be Edward Stratheru ; none save he
Could with my lost love at that moment be.

XCI.

" Down to the water's edge an ozier bed
     Extended opposite the hollow oak.
To know the worst an anxious longing led
     Me to this spot, which would my presence cloak ;
So I crawl'd thither, overwhelm'd with dread
     That the first words my giddy sweetheart spoke,
Would, at a blow, dispel my life's illusion—
My fear was right—to all the sex confusion !

XCII.

" When I the margin of the stream had gain'd,
     Forth from my ambush I look'd on the pair.
Her fond expressions Alice had retain'd
     Perhaps, had she conjectur'd I was there;
But thinking then they unobserv'd remain'd,
     No epithet endearing did she spare;
Much, too, she blam'd herself for mental blindness,
That to me ever she'd evinced a kindness.

XCIII.

" She sat—her head reposing on the breast
     Of her seducer, round her form whose arm
Was clasp'd—which gently the slight figure press'd,
     As tho' enchanted with some fairy's charm;
And well might motionless young Strathern rest!
     Kept in that loving posture by alarm,
Lest, by a movement, he should drive away
From his embrace that beauteous rustic fay.

XCIV.

" Her blue eyes look'd up lovingly to his,
     As if her soul were centred in their fire,
And gazing on that handsome face were bliss
     So exquisite she'd willingly expire
In its enjoyment. Then a burning kiss,
     Expressive of his glowing heart's desire,
Young Edward press'd upon her lips. I fell
Prone on the ground at this—I was in Hell.

XCV.

" Long time in stupor I remain'd, a prey
     To such wild agony it well-nigh burst
My aching heart; and when that pass'd away,
     In accents low most bitterly I curst
Alice, myself, and her deceiver gay,
     For whom I madly had affection nurs'd.
Time flitted on unnotic'd—years it seem'd
Had glided by me since of love I dream'd.

XCVI.

" But when I rose again, my misery
    With its intensity my heart appall'd ;
I felt alone on earth ; 'twas luxury
    The anguish that my wounded spirit gall'd
Was not observ'd by any curious eye,
    At last my fortitude in aid I call'd ;
And as 'twas midnight, in the fields I strode,
'Till the first purple light of morning shew'd.

XCVII.

" Exhausted then upon a cock of hay
    I sank, and fell into a troubled sleep.
I know not how long slumb'ring there I lay,
    But when I woke, an icy cold did creep
My limbs along ; while shooting pains did play
    Athwart my temples.   Wanting power to weep,
My hot eyes felt like cinders, and my brain
Whirl'd in a chaos with conceptions vain.

XCVIII.

" I rose ;—my stagg'ring limbs refus'd their aid.
    Down on the hay again half fainting, weak,
I sank—at my condition sore dismay'd,
    For how was I assistance there to seek ?
'Twas true of death I'd ceas'd to be afraid,
    Could I its presence instantly bespeak ;
But to lie lingering there in slow decay,
Was far too horrible—I must away.

XCIX.

" Hope was extinct in me ; and yet I strain'd
    Each muscle of my much exhausted frame,
Tho' ev'ry movement of my body pain'd
    Me so acutely that it overcame
My powers of endurance, ere I gain'd
    The distant stile, to reach which was my aim,
So that, with agony intense oppress'd,
I, three times, was compell'd to pause for rest.

C.

" Hope was extinct in me, then so I thought,
      But now how false the notion was, I know—
Hope *never* is extinct, howe'er distraught
      With misery men may fancy it is so ;
Hope *never* is extinct : its hues are caught
      E'en by the dying, and with promise glow ;
Hope *never* is extinct ; for hope is God,
The good man beckoning with approving nod.

CI.

" Hope *never* is extinct, save when the mind
      Has lost its balance, and calm reason reels
From men with feelings morbidly inclined,
      Hope, with her radiance, Black Despair conceals,
Then—But altho' insanity is blind,
      Hope none the less with smiling eye appeals
To suffering mortals—it may be in vain—
To lose all hope is to become insane.

CII.

" I gain'd the stile at length, and waited there,
      In expectation that some passer by
Would to my friends my helpless state declare ;
      And presently a man I knew drew nigh,
To whom some tale I told, with truthful air,
      So that he left me, with a pitying sigh,
To seek a vehicle for my removal—
A course to which I faintly gave approval.

CIII.

" He presently return'd with horse and cart,
      Bringing my mother also, in deep grief—
For, that he might prevail on her to start
      In search of me, he told her his belief
That I was dying, which she took to heart,
      And hurried to me to afford relief—
Having a vehicle contriv'd to borrow
Of one who pitied her maternal sorrow.

CIV.

" They rais'd me from the stile where I was sitting,
 And my form gently laid upon some straw
Within the vehicle, as was befiting
 For one so weak and helpless as they saw
I was become; our neighbour then us quitting,
 The horse excited his strange load to draw.
My aching head my mother's knees supported,
While she look'd sorrowing on my face distorted.

CV.

" And so we reach'd our home, when I was stripped
 And put to bed, with all convenient speed.
About the chamber then my mother tripp'd
 In search of ev'rything which I might need ;
By her advice I wine and water sipp'd ;
 Meanwhile our friend, upon the borrow'd steed,
Started to fetch the doctor—thinking still
That I was dying, and past human skill.

CVI.

" This I remember.—Then there came a blank
 In my existence.—Save that frightful dreams
Oppressed the sleep, disturbed to which I sank,
 The horrid images, delirium teems
Upon the fever'd brain—the brook's green bank—
 The hollow oak beneath the moon's pale beams ;
Alice expiring—while her fiend-like lover
Looked on triumphant—o'er my couch did hover.

CVII.

" To what deep withering curses I gave vent,
 While frenzied thus I lay ; I never knew,
My incoherent ravings closely pent
 Within her bosom, giving her a clue
To my wild agony, and how I'd spent
 The night in which my burning fever grew
My mother kept, and wisely, for e'en now
The mem'ry of my suff'ring wrings my brow.

CVIII.

" At last I woke to reason, but so weak,
　　And thin, and pale, with illness I had grown,
That for some days, when I essay'd to speak,
　　Was scarcely audible the falt'ring tone,
Which to convey my thoughts did feebly seek,
　　But vainly, dwindling to a piteous moan.
In fact the doctor boldly made assertion,
Death would ensue from any o'er exertion.

CIX.

" Time glided on, and with it health returned,
　　Of body—but my mind was prostrate laid.
Society of every kind I spurn'd,
　　And thro' the lanes and fields alone I stray'd ;
Within my bosom thoughts of vengeance burn'd,
　　Which should be sure, however long delay'd.
Alice had left the village with her lover,
It was supposed—tho' no one could discover.

CX.

" During my sickness ev'ry kindness shew'd
　　The 'Squire and Mrs. Strathern, but from me
The source from which the many comforts flow'd,
　　Above our means, I did around us see,
Was kept a secret—for with ire I glow'd
　　At Strathern's name, I from it's sound did flee.
I had determined ne'er again to take
My place, but rather home and friends forsake.

CXI.

" The autumn wan'd.　November dull and drear,
　　Came with its rain and fogs upon the land,
Clothing with sombre garb th' expiring year,
　　Bestowing on poor man, with cruel hand,
Those pains rheumatic, of old age the fear,
　　To guard against which are specifics plann'd,
Made—I have tried them, and can therefore tell,
Like Hodge's razors, with a view to sell.

CXII.

" Agaiu I was compell'd to keep the house,
  And so to books long-shunn'd I had recourse,
On which my sadden'd mind did idly browse,
  Acquiring still, each day, some added force ;
Till, from my state lethargic, I did rouse
  Myself, and in improvement found resource ;
But still revengeful feelings fill'd my heart,
Which black designs did to my mind impart.

CXIII.

" An open-hearted, wild and romping boy,
  A few short months had chang'd into a man,
Determined, desperate, anxious to destroy
  The villain who had marr'd the cherish'd plan
Of his existence—in his cup of joy
  The poison-drops to pour who'd first began—
Full many a scheme I form'd revenge to gain.
I shrank from *murder*, yet I wish'd him slain.

CXIV.

" 'Twas thus the winter moodily I pass'd.
  With spring return'd my health, my strength increas'd—
And from my thraldom I was freed at last,
  Glad, as a pris'ner is to be releas'd.
For some employment then around I cast
  My eyes ; for weaken'd had not been the least
My strong determination to resume,
No more my place as 'Squire Strathern's groom.

CXV.

" A mile or two from Stourton, in the vale,
  Where the canal pursued its sluggish course,
A public-house there stood, for its strong ale
  Far-fam'd, of many a bloody fray the source ;
When here, one eve, I did myself regale,
  A boatman having stopp'd to bait his horse,
Enter'd the kitchen, and our conversation
Decided then my future destination.

CXVI.

"Tall was he, and ungainly, and raw-bon'd,
    Of dark complexion, and of visage grim—
His mode of greeting not the least aton'd
    For what of ugliness you saw in him—
We took a pot together, and I moan'd
    Over the idleness that then did dim
My prospects, while, all silently he listen'd
To my sad tale, at which his black eyes glisten'd.

CXVII.

"'Cheer up, my lad,' said he—'I'll find you work.
    The man whom I employ'd has cut his stick,
Because he was too fond at nights to lurk
    In the preserves, the pheasants off to pick.
You seem a likely chap—not one to shirk
    Hard labour—nor your master play a trick.
If you will join me, I'll stay here to night,
And shall expect you with the morning's light!'

CXVIII.

"'I'll do so,' I responded, and we took,
    To bind the bargain then, a parting pot;
I left him smoking in the chimney nook,
    And started promptly for my father's cot.
I could not leave, without a parting look
    At my poor mother, whom I ne'er forgot.
Besides, I wanted clothing to equip me,
Ere with my new employer I could ship me.

CXIX.

"The night was fine as briskly out I stepp'd.
    My heart once more beat with a secret pleasure.
I wish'd to reach my home before they slept,
    And so the distance with all speed did measure.
For me I knew, my mother, vigils kept.
    My mother! (Ah! she was indeed a treasure)
I found her up. To bed was gone my father,
A circumstance that I was glad of, rather.

CXX.

" I told her I had met with Jemmy Gum,
    (Such was my master's short and ugly name!)
And that with him I'd bargain'd to become
    A Boatman, if to her 'twas all the same.
I thought she look'd, as this I told her, glum,
    But from her lips there no objection came ;
With all dispatch my bundle she adjusted,
And said 'To see me soon again she trusted.'

CXXI.

" And then we parted.   Down to the canal
    I took my way again to join my master—
He had been drinking in the interval,
    And when I reach'd him, thicker talk'd, and faster—
In fact, he was so drunk, he did appal
    Me, lest to him should happen a disaster
Ere we could gain the boat; but safely quite,
I manag'd there to stow him for the night.

CXXII.

" I woke by daylight, and the boat-horse sought,
    Which was, in truth, a very sorry hack,
By Jemmy at the coal-pits lately bought,
    And his old gear I fitted to his back.
(Him not worth provender I should have thought,
    Abraded was his hide by many a thwack,
But the boat he haul'd well), and then proceeded
To rouse my master, who a head-ache pleaded.

CXXIII.

" So in his cabin he remain'd, while I,
    Fast to the towing-rope the horse attach'd,
And gaily started my new trade to try,
    Whipping the old horse till he fairly snatch'd
With a long tug, from where it late did lie,
    The boat, and having then my motions watch'd,
Slack'ning his pace, more slowly onward wended,
Not thinking I perhaps to him attended.

K

CXXIV.

" But soon again I made him feel my thong.
　　On which he pull'd more strenuously than ever,
Tugging our craft most gloriously along,
　　And flagging in his great exertions never.
From sleep occasioned by potations strong,
　　Himself, my master, just contriv'd to sever,
At noon, and set himself to cook our dinner,
A task he said too hard for a beginner.

CXXV.

"I can assure you I was tir'd when night
　　Releas'd me from th' unusual exercise
In which I had engag'd since morning's light,
　　And sleep came quickly o'er my heavy eyes
When in the cabin, almost with delight,
　　Too small, alas! for two of our size,
I stow'd myself with Jemmy Gum, whose snoring
Like a struck Grampus sounded, aid imploring.

CXXVI.

" The next day we reached Oxford, and our load
　　Of coals discharg'd, and took in one of corn.
Back to the pits returning, as the mode
　　Was of the trade my master, did adorn ;
So much of zeal and aptitude I shew'd,
　　That, ere the summer months away had worn,
With Jemmy Gum I was become a fav'rite,
Because, he said " I knew how to behave right."

CXXVII.

" I must observe that Jem's idea of ' 'haviour'
　　(For so he call'd it, knowing nought of letters),
Was not a moral code to prove the saviour
　　Of any youth from vice's iron fetters ;
For he was just the very man to crave your
　　Society, to mix with the abettors
Of cock-fights, dog-fights, drunken brawls and poaching,
Which latter he thought not on right encroaching.

CXXVIII.

" And as for Drunkenness, it was not wrong
 In Jemmy's code of Ethics. By example
This he evinc'd, for with potations strong,
 Nightly himself he fuddl'd—tho' so ample
His powers of absorption were, that long
 He could drink with impunity. A sample
He was in fact of your well-season'd sot,
Who ev'ry morning wakes with ' copper's hot.' "

CXXIX.

" Stop, Adam," cried the Major, " so pathetic
 Your tale has been, my bottle's empty, quite—
The glass I'm drinking's nearly an emetic,
 So weak the toddy is. As young's the night,
And long your story, or I'm not prophetic,
 Some whiskey I must have—Go fetch it, *White*."
(*So* the old soldier did his nigger call,
Because no doubt he was not *white* at all).

CXXX.

With great alacrity the man obey'd ;
 And soon another bottle grac'd the table,
Which, when the Major had with care survey'd,
 He did uncork, as fast as he was able ;
To fill our glasses not to be afraid
 He told us then—but make us sociable ;
When with attention list'ning, we could sit,
To Adam's tale, while he concluded it.

CXXXI.

Old Adam filled his noggin—I my glass—
 We supp'd with gusto the refreshing mixture,
The rest the native liquor round did pass,
 Their keg not suffering to be a fixture.
And here my Canto ends— If it, alas !
 With anything of tediousness afflicts your
Attention, gentle reader, close the book,
I will essay your want of taste to brook.

END OF CANTO V.

CANTO VI.

—

I.

OLD Adam thus resum'd—" All kinds of vice
   I soon was made familiar with.   At first
It shock'd my young mind—but become less nice,
   I for excitement felt a burning thirst,
And so, at once, when broken was the ice
   Of virtue—in delirium accurst,
I plung'd into the abyss of dissipation,
With many others of my age and station.

II.

" And I drank hard, and with loud voice blasphem'd,
   Almost like Jem, my master in these arts.
But altho' joyous I to others seem'd,
   The mood came o'er me but by fits and starts—
As I have seen the sun when it has gleam'd
   In autumn weather—Gladness it imparts—
But soon the dark clouds gathering o'er us frown,
As if prepar'd again the world to drown.

III.

" Just so with me. My melancholy hours
   After a burst of mirth, with tenfold gloom,
Darken'd my mind.   The wounded heart devours,
   Like midnight ghouls in banquet o'er a tomb,
Its woes with madd'ning pleasure, and o'erpowers
   Each joy which lighten might the weight of doom.
The ' worm which dieth not ' already feeds
Upon the bosom that in secret bleeds.

IV.

" I must confess, upon the verge of crime
    I stood, like one upon a mountain's brow,
Rugged and stern, in loneliness sublime,
    Gazing ecstatic on the depths below—
A plunge were utter ruin in my prime,
    And yet the wish to plunge did on me grow—
I hail'd destruction with a wild delight,
For it methought would drown my mem'ry quite.

V.

" My occupation too afforded leisure
    For brooding o'er my hopeless misery.
Guarding my dark thoughts like a hidden treasure,
    I walk'd the path along, while many a sigh
Told that for me in life had gone all pleasure ;
    So day on day and month on month roll'd by ;
I knew each tract which border'd on my journey,
As well as legal quibbles an attorney.

VI.

" And when the boat was stopp'd at night, we went,
    I and my master, and some other men,
The evening who with us carousing spent,
    Poaching—for winter on was drawing then,
And the pale moon-beams their assistance lent
    Us, in the trees the pheasant tribes to ken.
With blacken'd faces and air-guns we sought 'em,
And down from where they sat in silence brought 'em.

VII.

" I visited my mother when we pass'd
    The spot which lay the nearest to my home.
She saw, poor woman, I was sinking fast
    In vice's whirlpool, and was then become
Deaf to all counsel, so she ceas'd, at last,
    From chiding me because I lov'd to roam
Instead of working quietly like others—
Sad thoughts indeed about me were my mother's.

VIII.

" One day as I was walking from the boat
     Up to the hamlet, riding at full speed,
I saw a horseman, but could only note
     As he pass'd on, his slender form agreed
With that of Edward Strathern ; but his throat
     Was muffled so, and with such haste his steed
He urg'd, that I could not observe his face ;
He seem'd howe'er to sit his horse with grace.

IX.

" Oh ! how I long'd to ride upon the wind,
     That I might overtake my deadly foe ;
Within my breast my vengeful heart repined,
     That then I could not slay him at a blow ;
I was determined, could I, out to find,
     If it my quondam master were or no ;
And therefore diligent enquiry made,
During the short time I, at Stourton, staid.

X.

" I found he then was living with the 'Squire,
     But not a word of Alice could I learn.
He'd wrought her ruin, so she lost desire
     Amongst her friends and kindred to return.
Perhaps she was deserted, now the fire
     Of his hot passion did no longer burn.
Loving him madly, trusting in his truth,
She was destroy'd, abandon'd in her youth.

XI.

" I tried to plan some scheme by which I might
     Avenge her fate on her seducer's head—
This was my thought by day, my dream by night,
     As with the boat to Oxford on I sped—
It almost seem'd a duty to requite
     Wrong for the wound from which I daily bled.
Too soon, alas ! a most unlucky chance
Did my fell purpose to its aim advance.

XII.

" I've said the 'Squire was a stout preserver
 Of game, and hated poachers more than sin,
Whom he pursued with such impetuous fervor,
 As would have made a very stoic grin,
If of the actions he'd been an observer
 With which old Strathern frighted all his kin.
He watch'd at nights with guns and pistols loaded,
When he a trespass on his grounds foreboded.

XIII.

" And once or twice engag'd in an affray
 With his inveterate foes he'd got a bruising ;
Which him, however, snug in bed to stay,
 Did not induce, but while yet sore, abusing
The poaching rascals, threat'ning to repay
 Them with three month's imprisonment for using
Their cudgels on his carcase, to his surgeon
He grumbled, of the grave the very verge on.

XIV.

" Then, being recover'd, hot again for action,
 Just like Don Quixote when he'd been o'erthrown,
He soon was busy stopping an infraction
 Of the Game-laws by methods all his own ;
And it was well, if in this new transaction
 He'd not again a beating to bemoan.
So his son Edward fill'd him with delight,
When he had shot a poacher in a fight.

XV.

" We long had look'd upon the 'Squire's preserves
 As well worth visiting, should we remain
A night, where, sweeping in successive curves,
 The canal border'd on his wide domain
My master, Jemmy, was a man whose nerves
 Were far too strong for any fear of pain
To shake—and so he loudly swore ' od rot him,'
He'd have some pheasants if th' old fellow shot him.

XVI.

" When we return'd from Oxford, near the inn—
    The inn where Jem and I at first had met—
We stopp'd the boat, and tippling did begin,
    With other twain before the sun did set ;
And while we drank our beer, the house within,
    Inspir'd to valour by our ' heavy wet,'
We all determin'd on an expedition
Against the pheasants, e'en if 'twere perdition.

XVII.

" It was a moonlight night—we curs'd that moon—
    A dark one would have serv'd our purpose better ;
But still we might not find occasion soon
    T' effect our end, did we permit to fetter
Us times or seasons.   I believe at noon
    We then had sallied forth without regret or
Fear—for with ale we were become uproarious,
And thought a scuffle would be something glorious.

XVIII.

" With guns and bludgeons, we proceeded, arm'd,
    In search of game ; and in contempt of law,
Not in the least deter'd, or e'en alarm'd,
    Altho' the keepers, going their rounds, we saw.
At any other time I had been charm'd
    With the bright scene ; after a few hours' thaw
The frost again was hardening the ground,
While rul'd the night a silence most profound.

XIX.

" Skulking behind a hedge, we kept on guard,
    Whilst the three keepers went their evening rounds,
Which from our sport did us some time retard,
    Because until had died away the sounds
Of their retiring feet, we were debarr'd
    From ent'ring unobserv'd the 'Squire's grounds
But when the course was clear, we climb'd a gate
Into a wood, led on, I think by fate.

XX.

" The keepers we had seen, I recoguized,
    Tho' we, it seem'd, were not observ'd by them ;
Being thus of all th' opposing force appris'd,
    Precaution p'rhaps we did too much contemn.
True, each like Blackey's, had his face disguised,
    But still we talked—a practice I condemn—
And laugh'd, too, loudly, treating as *diversion*,
What prov'd to all a *serious* excursion.

XXI.

" Those who have never poach'd, have yet to feel
    The wild delight which its excitement yields ;
'Tis glorious thro' the woods at night to steal,
    Or briskly glide across the moonlit fields ;
'Tis glorious, thinking of your morrow's meal,
    A plump cock-pheasant, which some light bough shields,
To shoot, as he unwarily exposes
His gorgeous plumage, moving as he doses.

XXII.

" 'Tis glorious sometimes too, to have a fray
    With sturdy keepers, who oppose your sport,
Provided you are not compelled to slay,
    But only to hard cudgelling resort ;
'Tis true from justice you must slink away,
    Too apt to crime your pastime to distort ;
But 'tis a pleasure even to escape
From the law's clutches, when you're in a scrape.

XXIII.

" Perhaps we'd been an hour on the scout,
    Bagging some twenty pheasants in the time,
When we began to think of getting out
    Of the preserves ; so that, ere morning's prime,
Far down ' the cut ' in safety, beyond doubt,
    Chuckling at our success, with joy sublime,
We might to each his share of game allot,
After we'd gain'd some snug, secluded spot.

XXIV.

" But here our fortune fail'd us.   There arose
    Upon our ear the sound of steps approaching,
Which could not friendly be—nay, would be foes,
    Who came to punish us for our encroaching ;
We must prepare us for immediate blows—
    Nothing uncommon when one is out poaching ;
And so of coppice-wood we gain'd a thicket,
Determin'd there, on watch, to form a picket.

XXV.

" We squatted down, in readiness to rise,
    And fight for freedom and our slaughter'd game,
If towards our lurking-place they cast their eyes,
    Who to oppose our quiet exit came.
Like Indian warriors group'd for a surprise,
    Silent, unmoving, but with hearts of flame,
Our weapons ready, and our eyes alert,
To view the first who should the coppice skirt.

XXVI.

" I was the outward man ; and soon descried
    Approaching thro' the wood, with cautious tread,
Those we expected, who themselves applied
    To search each clump of trees, whose branches spread,
So that they did a lurking-place provide—
    The 'Squire himself was marching at their head ;
Another, too, had join'd the keepers three,
Young Edward Strathern, it appear'd to me.

XXVII.

" Now was the moment come, my soul desir'd.
    Vengeance long thirsted for would soon be mine ;
I well nigh pointed then my gun and fir'd,
    But paus'd, relinquishing this first design ;
The party who were seeking us, retir'd,
    As the thought flash'd on me, and did incline
Towards a more distant part of the plantation,
Which movement we regarded with elation.

XXVIII.

Already we suppos'd ourselves secure,
  And deem'd the hour of danger had pass'd by,
But this impression turn'd out premature,
  For just as we arose, prepar'd to fly,
Of our escape, and of our booty sure,
  The keepers and the squire again drew nigh.
This time they saw us, and resolv'd to capture.
To stand and yield, they hail'd us first, with rapture.

XXIX.

" My master, Jemmy, being now at bay,
  Responded to their summons in these words—
' My lads we are not anxiuos for a fray,
  Let us pass quietly, but take the birds—
That's what I call good usage and fair play ;
  Here in this game-bag that my body girds
Are six fine pheasants—take them every one,
But suffer us in safety to be gone.'

XXX.

" ' Not so,' the 'Squire reply made, with an oath,
  ' You must yield also, or we mean to take you.
You, and your pheasants, we are sure of both,
  Lay your arms down, or we will quickly make you ;
To fire upon your party I am loth,
  But must do so—to reason to awake you—
Yield then, my lads, your conduct's indefensible,
Of which I'm sure all of you are quite sensible.'

XXXI.

" ' We'll see you d—'d first,' shouted all in chorus,
  ' Take us, if take you can, but no child's play
You'll find it,' added Jemmy. ' From before us
  Remove your men, that we may go away,
Or, by the mothers who in sorrow bore us,
  We'll fire, determin'd or to maim or slay.'
And each his air gun, at a foe directed,
To shoot if he advanc'd, as we expected.

XXXII.

" There was a pause.—The old man stood aghast,
    He had imagined we should yield at once ;
Some hurried words amongst the party pass'd,
    Then to their shoulders they applied their guns.
    Yield, or we fire,—this warning is the last,'
    Exclaim'd the 'Squire. ' I'll shoot the first that runs,'
Jem plac'd us all secure behind the bushes,
Then shouted ' death to him who forward rushes.'

XXXIII.

" I aim'd at Edward,—took deliberate aim,
    Ah ! how for vengeance did my spirit groan,
And deadly hatred thrill'd my quiv'ring frame !
    That moment should for all my wrongs atone,
And wipe away in blood my darling's shame.
    Upon the group in all her glory shone
The moon, whose beams along each barrel glanced—
They fir'd a volley—and on us advanced.

XXXIV.

" At first they were obscur'd by the smoke.
    But soon that drifted upward. On our view,
Ere they the coppice reach'd, their figures broke.
    A murderous fire we on them rushing threw.
Their's had pass'd harmless, serving to provoke
    The deadly conflict which did then ensue.
But nearly every ball we sent them told,
And on the ground two lifeless bodies roll'd.

XXXV.

" There yet were left to struggle the old 'Squire,
    And Edward Strathern, who'd receiv'd a wound,
Which stung him all the more to vent his ire
    In levelling those who'd shot him to the ground.
And the head-keeper, who'd reserv'd his fire,
    So that he did us suddenly astound,
By shooting poor Tom Wallis thro' the head,
Who roll'd a moment, and then fell stone-dead.

XXXVI.

" We now were three to three. When ' Greek meets Greek
     Then comes the tug of war,' I've often heard.
With courage truly Grecian, we did seek
     Each other's downfall.—It by chance occurr'd
That Edward aim'd at me, prepar'd to wreak
     My vengeance on him—vengeance long deferr'd,
A blow,—which by good luck, was render'd vain.
I parried it, or surely had been slain.

XXXVII.

" Ere he recover'd, and while stooping yet,
     Straining my ev'ry muscle for the blow,
With one fell swoop, I paid my heavy debt,
     Laying my enemy for ever low.
My fiendlike feelings I shall ne'er forget,
     When full upon the temple of my foe,
My cudgel struck ; immediately prone
He sank, and, shivering, died without a groan.

XXXVIII.

" Thus was a mother's hopes—a mother's pray'rs
     Made futile at a stroke—a righteous stroke ;
For, when I think, my judgment now declares
     That retribution upon him who broke
A young and trusting heart, which black despair's
     Madness induced destruction to invoke;
Which made a timid girl—in sin's abyss,
Resort to suicide as almost bliss.

XXXIX.

" That retribution was the work of God, *
     No matter how this hand may reek with crime,
Which wielded, sinning, the avenging rod,
     Nerv'd with the deadliest hatred at the time ;
And when I shall be laid beneath the sod,
     In a land distant from my native clime,
What man Heaven's judgment can pretend to tell,
On him who murder'd, and on him who fell.

---

* The Author begs to observe that these opinions are Mr. Adam Faber's—
not his.

XL.

"Murder!   There's something startling in the sound!
    But still we met in fight, my hand prevail'd ;
Had I his equal been, I could have found
    A thousand pretexts him to have assail'd—
Nor would the world upon the deed have frown'd,
    Of one of these had I myself avail'd,
And shot him fashionably with a second.
Then the affair most glorious had been reckon'd.

XLI.

"This hand is red with blood—I saw him lie
    Extended there beneath the waning moon.
Extinguished was the fire of that dark eye,
    Whose smiling glance almost conferr'd a boon.
The blood ooz'd from his temple lazily.
    Was it grim death indeed, or but a swoon?
I stoop'd and felt his heart—it did not beat,
He was a corpse, and my revenge complete.

XLII.

"A moment's triumph follow'd the black deed,
    Then, which has never left me since, remorse
Made me regret it was not mine to bleed
    On that dread night, on which I had recourse,
The first and only time, as fate decreed,
    In wreaking vengeance, to aggressive force.
Years have elapsed, but burning on my brow,
I feel the brand of Cain—now, even now."

XLIII.

Old Adam paus'd, and down each furrowed cheek
    There roll'd hot tears, while sobs convuls'd his frame ;
He tried, and tried again in vain to speak,
    But no words from his lips distorted came.
Emotions long pent up had pow'r to wreak
    Their fury, fann'd to a devouring flame.
His face he covered with his sinewy hand,
Hiding the torrent he could not command.

XLIV.

We silent sat, respecting his deep grief.
    The Major mov'd, uneasy, in his chair ;
Then sought to give his servitor relief,
    By him assuring with a serious air,
Himself, if he were worthy of belief,
    Had slain some dozens without thought or care.
" To kill a man in fight, and call it murder,"
Concluded he—" I ne'er heard aught absurder.

XLV.

" Just calm yourself a little, Adam, will you ?
    And take a glass of grog before proceeding—
The liquor's good, and cannot fail to still you,
    For a consoler you are truly needing—
There —there—that's right, don't let your feelings kill you,
    And, when you're ready we'll be after heeding
Your story strange, which fills us all with wonder.
Cheer up—To slay that youth was no great blunder."

XLVI.

' Old Adam soon grew calmer, and narrated
    The sequel of his story—as ensues—
" If I remember, I've already stated,
    That three to three we did our weapons use,—
The 'Squire took Jem, nor were they separated,
    Until the former sore with many a bruise
Fell to the earth ; while Jack our friend—the keeper,
Made till the judgment day shall come, a sleeper.

XLVII.

" He then proceeded to inspect his wounded,
    And we fled hastily beyond the wood—
Over the fencing, then like moose-deer bounded,
    Nor, till we'd gain'd the open meadows, stood.
As here the prospect was well nigh unbounded,
    We look'd to see if any one pursued ;
But finding no one following, more at leisure,
Tow'rds the canal we did the distance measure.

XLVIII.

" Into a ditch as on we passed, we threw
　　The pheasants, we had at such risk obtain'd,
And burnt our clothing, to destroy all clue
　　To our identity, when we had gain'd
The boat; and, still afraid they should pursue,
　　No long time there inactive we remain'd;
But fetch'd our horse, and, ere the break of day,
Were many miles along the 'cut' away.

XLIX.

" I drove the horse, and as I trudg'd along,
　　A whirl of wild thoughts darted on my brain,
To which altho' I strove, resistance strong
　　To offer—Yet, alas! I strove in vain.
The fearful details of the past did throng
　　Upon my mind—The image of the slain,
As there he lay a corpse—his glassy eye
Accusing me that he so young did die.

L.

" ——The hasty flight—the consciousness of guilt,
　　The dire reproaches of life-long remorse—
The horror which I felt at having spilt
　　Blood;—and the future to my view seem'd worse.
Dreading detection—' Go where ere thou wilt,'
　　I said, myself addressing—' no resource
Thou hast—the avenging angel is behind,
And retribution thou art sure to find.'

LI.

" ——The seizure, the imprisonment, the trial,
　　The crowded court, the judge's angry frown,
The accusation, and the faint denial
　　Of crime, 'twere almost better to avow.
My heart was harden'd, but could not defy all
　　These sad impressions—natural, you'll allow.
Then came the verdict, and the gallows loom'd.
I felt a murd'rer, and a murd'rer doom'd.

LII.

"We reach'd the coal-pits—where the news had spread
　　Of the affray which Jem and I surviv'd.
The guilty parties, 'twas supposed, had fled ;
　　T' elude all search they'd certainly contriv'd.
Five men were left in the plantation, dead,
　　And of all sense the 'Squire was depriv'd.
The weekly papers a description glowing,
Gave of the conflict, with lies overflowing.

LIII.

"And a reward was offered.　On the walls
　　Huge placards met my half-averted eye.
With inward trembling I obey'd the calls
　　To labour, dreading every passer by.
Oh! how the spirit conscious guilt enthrals,
　　Making one shrink and crouch, and skulk and fly.
Had the earth open'd to receive me then,
It had been joy—t' escape from human ken.

LIV.

"But no suspicion was attached to us.
　　The constables were hunting every town,
And making idly a tremendous fuss,
　　Scouring the country round, both up and down.
The magistrates held meetings to discuss
　　The means by which success might surely crown
The search for those the dreadful deed who'd done,
Who'd bruis'd their comrade—slain his only son.

LV.

"Sev'ral unlucky men were apprehended
　　Who were as innocent 'as babes unborn,'
And when examinations had extended,
　　Touching their guilt, whole morning after morn,
The while, they being entirely unbefriended,
　　Were from their families unjustly torn
And kept in prison—they were sent away,
Suspicion clinging to them many a day.

L

LVI.

" But all was vain.   The keeper and the 'Squire
　　Could not identify their midnight foes ;
They scarcely saw the latter, ere the fire
　　Pour'd from their guns, and when they came to blows.
So were they blinded by infuriate ire,
　　They sought but on the enemy to close.
They knew not whether they were short or tall,
Who'd struggled with them—lucky not to fall.

LVII.

" Meanwhile, my master Jem and I agreed,
　　To work the boat till summer should come round,
And then with all haste possible proceed,
　　Refuge to seek on Transatlantic ground.
Strict silence we preserv'd, of which we'd need,
　　For angry justice on our persons frown'd.
Our coals we loaded, and tow'rds Oxford started,
Fearing to be arrested—heavy hearted.

LVIII.

" We did not stop the boat to spend the night,
　　Where in our voyage down it had remain'd,
When we involv'd were in that mortal fight,
　　In which our hands with bloodshed had been stain'd :
But saw the landlord of the inn, whose plight
　　Resembl'd our's, tho' he indiff'rence feign'd.
He said there was no danger of detection,
If we were influenced by circumspection.

LIX.

" And so for months we carried on our trade,
　　Jem, shunning, prudently, intoxication ;
Which him, perhaps, might garrulous have made,
　　And hinder'd our dark secret's preservation.
I must confess that I was sore afraid,
　　Whenever he indulg'd in conversation
Over his cups, lest he by chance should mention,
Facts which might justify our apprehension.

LX.

"But when the spring arriv'd, our fears grew less,
　I ventur'd then to call upon my mother;
I was embarrass'd, and by her distress,
　I saw she could not all suspicion smother.
We talk'd of Strathern's murder,—but more stress
　She laid not on that topic than another.
Yet in her moist eye there arose a tear,
Which spite of all her struggles would appear.

LXI.

"I dare not tell her then, I meditated
　Quitting my country, lest she should demand
The reason; so I long-time hesitated,
　Before acquainting her with what I'd plann'd.
But when the time approach'd, I shortly stated,
　'Twas my design to seek a foreign land;
That all my preparations were completed,
And for my passage I'd already treated.

LXII.

"The news came on her suddenly—She heav'd
　From her rent bosom an appalling sigh—
'Alone, deserted, in my age bereav'd,
　Forlorn and comfortless, I now must die.
I thought to see, ere me the grave receiv'd,
　A wife my place in your young heart supply.
I thought t' have clasp'd your children to my breast,
Then all in peace I could have sunk to rest.

LXIII.

"'But now, such joy for ever is denied.
　You flee your mother—your fond mother, flee—
Unconscious of what evils may betide
　You in the land which she can never see:
And should you perish—cut off in your pride,
　What grief, what agony, will cling to me.
I greatly fear there is some secret cause
For this decision—Pause, oh Adam! pause.'

LXIV.

" Thus spake she ; and the tears in torrents roll'd
    Down her wan cheeks.   She flew to my embrace,
And while her wither'd arms my form did fold,
    She gaz'd intently, wildly on my face.
My own emotion, struggling, I control'd ;
    But all my firmness banish'd for a space.
I nerv'd my heart—my mother pacified
At length, and thus to her outburst replied.

LXV.

" ' Mother ! I wish to God it could have been
    As you have dreamt ; but that forbids my fate.
I lov'd—how dearly—you yourself have seen ;
    You half suspect how I have wreak'd my hate.
I cannot tell the tale ; but one between
    Me and my happiness there was of late—
He perish'd ;—this right hand depriv'd of life
Young Strathern.   Can I think of child or wife ?

LXVI.

" ' And she whom I aveng'd—where is she ?   Gone
    Were she but dead ; in mourning o'er her tomb
Some consolation I might find alone
    Thus to be left, in manhood's early bloom ;
But, dead to me, she lives an outcast one.
    This shades my heart with a funereal gloom.
To virtue lost, to happiness, to me,
Is she whose memory I'm compell'd to flee.

LXVII.

" ' I must away.   My mother, do not weep,
    Or weep, if tears your aching heart relieve ;
Alas ! *my* agony is far too deep
    For even your fond bosom to conceive.
Quiet by day—by night untroubled sleep
    Can no more visit me.   Nay, do not grieve ;
Foully I've sinn'd ; but pardon for my crime
He will accord whose mercy is sublime.

LXVIII.

"'I must away; my mother dear, farewell!
  Again on earth we never more can meet;
If aught my lifelong misery could dispel,
  'Twould be thy smile in after years to greet;
But here we part for ever—do not dwell   .
  Upon a hope which time will surely cheat.
We part—we part! adieu! my mother dear,
May blessings flow upon you year by year.'

LXIX.

"A parting kiss upon her lips I press'd;
  Again her aged arms she round me flung;
Then, fainting, fell upon my tortur'd breast,
  Where with convulsive clasp she lifeless clung.
Her hold I loosen'd of her son unblest,
  And ere sensation was return'd, I sprung,
Sprung from her arms and from the house, away;—
We've never seen each other since that day.

LXX.

" I join'd my master, who was with the boat,
  And our last journey down the 'cut' we took,
Devising plans which should our end promote;
  Pausing to take, at times, a farewell look
At each familiar spot—the hills remote;
  And, thro' the fields, meand'ring, the glad brook:
The scatter'd villages—the well-known farms
Which broke upon us with a thousand charms.

LXXI.

" I have seen nature in her grandest forms—
  The rock, the lake, the forest, the cascade;
The ocean, frenzied by terrific storms,
  The desert praries expansive laid.
But none of these my mem'ry kindly warms,
  Like the sweet landscape Jem and I survey'd,
As slowly down the towing path we went,
On quitting England's shores for ever, bent.

LXXII.

" We reach'd the coal-pits, and discharg'd our load,
    Jem sold his horse and boat the following day ;
There, to arrange all matters, we abode
    A week ; and then to Liverpool our way
Pursued.   At that time coaches kept the road,
    Well hors'd, to obviate the least delay ;
We took our places upon one of these,
And soon were at th' emporium of the seas.

LXXIII.

" Our passage we had taken ere we came,
    But found the vessel not prepar'd to sail—
The 'Alligator' was its Yankee name ;
    The skipper said it ne'er was known to fail—
'Twould skim the waters over all the same,
    Whether 'twas calm or blew a boisterous gale.
For emigrants was fitted up the hold.
All the best berths were taken, we were told.

LXXIV.

" We chose our own ; and then a lodging sought ;
    We found a humble one, not distant far
From where the vessel was alongside brought,
    In Prince's Dock, resort of many a tar ;
To occupy our leisure we had nought
    But all the sights in Liverpool, which are,
The docks, the shipping, warehouses, exchange ;
Observing which, we thro' the town did range.

LXXV.

" One night as in the streets I saunter'd, sad,
    Thinking with sorrow on the gloomy past,
And gazing moodily upon the glad
    And restless crowd which glided by me fast,
I saw a girl, most elegantly clad,
    Walking the street, whom instantly I class'd
With those, the Pariahs of her sex, whose trade
Cannot to modest ears be well convey'd.

LXXVI.

" I follow'd her, for o'er me came a thrill,
    As tho' her fate were woven with my own—
I had no thought of doing any ill,
    For to all women I'd indiff'rent grown—
But there was something acting on my will
    Which led me on.—I'd stopp'd if I had known
Who that young creature was of glorious beauty,
Thus early straying from the path of duty.

LXXVII.

" She swept along the street with mincing gait,
    Assum'd t' attract the idle loungers there ;
And ever and anon she'd pause to wait
    For one who'd ey'd her with a sensual stare.
Then she her motions would accelerate,
    As if she hasted to arrive somewhere.
At length she met a gentleman, who wink'd,
And on they walk'd together closely link'd.

LXXVIII.

" They were some twenty yards before me then,
    And we had almost reach'd the termination
Of the long street, all on a sudden when
    They turn'd, indulging still in conversation ;
I stood beneath a lamp, and on my ken,
    The young girl's features, form'd for admiration
Gleam'd in the light, as she the pavement trod—
'Twas Alice—my own Alice—oh ! my God.

LXXIX.

" Her eye met mine ; she recognis'd my face,
    And wildly shrieking on the cold stone fell.
Her gay companion look'd around to trace
    The cause which made her suddenly unwell ;
Then gently raising her, contriv'd to place
    Her lifeless form—unable to repel
His assiduities, within the door
Of a gin-palace, and—I saw no more.

LXXX.

" I fled.   Along the streets I madly ran,
    Not knowing whither—till I reach'd the dock
Hatless, and out of breath.   I then began
    To pause, recov'ring somewhat from the shock
Which lately had come on me.   Should I scan
    Each night the streets, and those who there might flock.
To find my lost love, anxious to reclaim ?
Or should I leave her in her sin and shame ?

LXXXI.

" Was she aware of her seducer's fate ?
    She must have read of his mysterious end ;
Could I, whom she had fled, anticipate
    She would receive me as indeed a friend ?
Would she not shun me in her present state,
    E'en if success should on my search attend ?
Besides, she might suspect me—woman's heart
Oft on the truth instinctively will dart.

LXXXII.

" ' No ! I must never—never see her more !'
    I shouted wildly—' or my heart will break—
She who deserted me for sin before,
    Sin, at my instance will not now forsake—
And how can I approach her—when the gore
    Of him whose life it was my crime to take
Yet stains this hand—so that no water may
Have pow'r the damn'd spot e'er to cleanse away.

LXXXIII.

" I saunter'd by the dock-wall all the night—
    My mind a chaos of conflicting thought,
And reach'd my lodging as the morning light
    Th' horizon streaking I obscurely caught.
O'erwhelm'd with what I'd seen, and weary quite,
    Repose was welcome, so my bed I sought.
Kind Nature granted the desir'd boon,
And slumber held my senses until noon.

LXXXIV.

" Not many days we tarried after this—
  The emigrants arriv'd, the wind was fair ;
So that the skipper, anxious not to miss
  Th' occasion, bade us, with all speed, prepare—
To do which we were by no means remiss,
  And thus we join'd those who the ship did share.
Three hundred Irish stow'd between the decks,
Our voyage did with their disputing vex.

LXXXV.

" We clear'd the dock.—A steamer tow'd us down
  The river, and we gain'd the Irish Sea ;
The tug then left us—steering tow'rds the town ;
  The wind sufficing, from its aid when free,
To drive our vessel. Not a cloud did frown
  A bright fine morning as it chanc'd to be ;
And the sun, shining on the yeasty foam,
Appear'd to smile on us, deserting home.

LXXXVI.

Ours was a motley party—men and *boys,*
  Not *Irish boys*—but boys I mean in age—
Young women newly enter'd on the joys
  Of wedlock, which no sorrow did presage
Worse than their poverty. With constant noise,
  Loud-screaming infants did our ear engage—
Besides their grandmother's incessant chatter,
Fill'd all the 'tween decks with a tonguey clatter.

LXXXVII.

" As we sail'd down the channel—upon deck,
  T" escape the racket down below, we stay'd,
Eyeing intently each projecting neck
  Of land the lucid atmosphere display'd ;
The sailors, ever and anon, a speck,
  Far inland, which with int'rest we survey'd,
Shew'd us, and told us, both its situation
In either country, and its designation.

LXXXVIII.

" Along we scudded gaily all the day ;
      And the wind freshen'd as the evening clos'd,
Propelling us upon our wat'ry way ;
      So that the good ship made, as we repos'd,
A glorious run ; and, when, at morning grey,
      Again our persons we on deck expos'd,
Cape Clear was looming on our starboard-quarter.
Soon after, we were cutting thro' 'blue water.'

LXXXIX.

" Our berths below were by no means the best
      Couches whereon a weary man could lie ;
The noise prevented anything like rest ;
      Of infants there was an incessant cry.
The stench, like that which propagates a pest,
      Induc'd us from its influence to fly.
The women quarrell'd, and the men blasphem'd,
While others snor'd sonorous as they dream'd.

XC.

" All days on board a ship are much the same,
      You rise and cook your breakfast—take your tea—
Then walk the deck, till your attention claim
      What preparations seem to you to be
Expedient (or you are much to blame),
      Your dinner to prepare : for, when at sea,
Each steerage passenger must dress his own,
Or, want of food he's likely to bemoan.

XCI.

" Your dinner taken, you must walk again
      The vessel's deck, till time for tea comes round ;
Talking and idly gazing on the main,
      And list'ning to the water's splashing sound ;
When the sun sets in glory you are fain
      To seek your berth ; and, if in slumber bound,
The night will pass more rapidly away,
Than does th' unvaried, endless-seeming day.

XCII.

" Our passage was propitious.   Off th' Azores,
   Tow'rds the south driven by a north-east gale,
We were becalm'd a day or two, where pours
   The sun a glowing heat.   Each rag of sail
Was useless there.   Then tow'rds the western shores
   A strong east wind did steadily prevail,
So that our vessel soon approach'd New York,
Having most gallantly perform'd her work.

XCIII.

" In eight-and-twenty days we reach'd the quay,
   And landed—each elated with the hope
That in the New World, from the troubles free,
   With which in Europe he was forced to cope,
A prosp'rous future he would surely see,
   And for his talents find sufficient scope.
Our Irish friends proceeded tow'rds the west.
To tarry at New York to us seem'd best.

XCIV.

" I shall not dwell upon my early days
   Of Transatlantic life.   I wrote a letter
Home to my mother, which I thought would raise
   Her spirits; telling her my chance was better
In the New World; for there were various ways
   Of seeking fortune there, to whom a debtor
I ne'er had been.   Of Alice I said nought,
Tho' of her sad state constantly I thought.

XCV.

" Jem parted from me in a week or two.
   He could not find employment in the city,
And, tir'd of having nought at all to do,
   He said ' to waste his life there seem'd a pity ' —
And when I told him I should get work.   ' Pooh! '
   Was his reply—but did not intermit I
My search for labour, which when I'd obtain'd,
No longer living near me he remain'd—

XCVI.

" But travell'd West. I've never seen him since.
  I've heard, however, in the Texan war
He did much skill and bravery evince,
  And, shining brightly as a border star,
From fighting Mexicans did never wince —
  His fame for valour there was spread afar ;
So that with laurels cover'd he retir'd
On a snug farm, by all his friends admir'd.

XCVII.

" I've said, I got employment.   As a groom
  I let myself to one who own'd a paper—
' The New York Smasher,' which, like a simoom,
  Those who against its articles did vapour,
O'erwhelm'd –regardless of their woeful doom ;
  In politics it cut full many a caper.
My master wrote with wonderful facility,
The world astonishing with his scurrility.

XCVIII.

" Thus I became acquainted with all news,
  And studied politics with great intensity.
I never coincided with the views
  Of my employer, owing to the density,
He hinted, of my skull ; and did abuse
  For all things British my perverse propensity.
In argument I often made him furious.
He said my prejudice was really curious.

XCIX.

" I took again to reading—books I mean—
  And gain'd much knowledge in my leisure hours.
I was not overwork'd ; and so between
  The times of my employment, I my pow'rs
Of thought improv'd.   My relish still is keen
  For this diversion, and my mind devours,
As Major Horner knows, each varied tome.
With England's authors I am quite at home.

C.

" But still I did not lose my sottish ways,
    And so my money went as it was earn'd ;
The habit I regret.—Too many praise
    A custom, they themselves, by chance have learn'd.
A drunkard I have been—have spent my days
    In mad intoxication, while I spurn'd
The baneful practice—now would gladly change,
But have not courage. This is strange—most strange.

CI.

" When at New York I'd been about a year,
    I heard of Alice—heard of her decease.
By her own hand she fell—to mem'ry dear.
    I hope, against belief, she sleeps in peace.
Remorse had struck her, and the growing fear
    That sorrow with the future would increase ;
And so she took a dose of prussic acid,
Which spoil'd in death, her face's beauty placid.

CII.

" Some men can love, and when the lov'd one dies,
    Their restless hearts can new affections weave ;
Not so with me.—The same cold grave where lies
    My buried love, my dead heart did receive.
Beauty in vain has glow'd upon these eyes,
    Now dim with age,—dimmer that I did grieve.
But never since upon my wither'd heart,
Has glanc'd for woman ought like passion's dart.

CIII.

" I lov'd but once—and on that love my all
    I ventur'd—losing. When the die was cast
My hopes of happiness at once did fall,
    And passion was a bright dream of the past.
I dar'd not strive the feeling to recall,
    And so my first affection was my last.
Alice, I lov'd—that love provok'd to guilt,
Forbad another, the red blood I spilt.

CIV.

" For five long years I tarried at New York,
    Grooming my master's horse, his leaders reading
And then, grown weary of continuous work,
    I thought of to the younger States proceeding
  To take a farm, and raise for export, pork,
    For there the pigs pay gloriously for feeding.
So one fine morning I inform'd the editor
The sum I needed, which made me his creditor.

CV.

" He paid me ; and with that supply of cash,
    I took the steam-boat, starting for the West ;
I was determin'd now to make a dash
    At fortune, and my scanty funds invest.
What I had heard of hardships to abash,
    Tended my hopes, which still were for the best. '
I steam'd to Albany, and then to Troy ;
Where as a groom again I found employ.

CVI.

" Here six months I remain'd.—Then in a boat
    For Buffalo, I started—which we made ;
When, in the Erie Canal afloat,
    I was reminded of my former trade ;
And scenes in England dearer, now remote,
    My longing mind discursively survey'd.
From Buffalo again I took a steamer,
Of thoro' Yankee build, and called the ' Screamer.'

CVII.

" In Indiana I procured a farm,
    With a log-hut, and everything complete ;
At first the solitude had power to charm,
    Not so the labour which requir'd my wheat.
I view'd my fields with something like alarm,
    Finding reality did fancy cheat.
Weary, for city life again I panted,
And so I sold my clearing, and levanted.

CVIII.

" While I was farming, my poor mother died ;
 The news was sent me by my sorrowing father ;
Her love for me death's agony defied ;
 She gave her blessing, which consol'd me rather.
Over her loss for many a day I sighed.
 In peace, she breath'd her last, as I could gather.
She never told her husband of my crime ;
Her fond affection was indeed sublime.

CIX.

" When I reach'd Buffalo, I looked about
 For work—but finding none to suit my views,
I was resolv'd in Canada to scout,
 Hoping that Fortune me would better use.
And so, I cross'd the Lake, but not without
 Experiencing a storm as we did cruise.
I went to Queenston, where Sir Isaac Brock,
Met death most nobly in the battle's shock.

CX.

" There I got work again, and tarried long.
 My master kept a store, and paid me well ;
So I conceived for him affection strong,
 And with him did most comfortably dwell.
He died, rememb'ring me his friends among—
 I staid till for him toll'd the funeral bell ;
Then to Toronto came, where Major Horner,
Was in the fort at that time a sojourner.

CXI.

" We scrap'd acquaintance ; and when he retir'd
 From active service, buying this estate ;
By him to groom his horses, I was hir'd.
 What has pass'd since, 'twere bootless to relate.
I've found my master all that I desir'd,
 And here my final summons I await.
My father's dead—relations I have none,
And so on earth I am alone—alone !"

CXII.

Old Adam ceas'd to speak. The Major started,
    For he had been indulging in a nap,
And tow'rds his toddy his right hand he darted,
    Which he upset. Aghast at the mishap,
He took another glass ; and thus imparted
    His thoughts on Adam's story " My old chap,
You've told your tale most ably, and with candour,
Not deigning from the main thread once to wander.

CXIII.

" We all have been most deeply interested
    In your adventures, and have sigh'd or smil'd,
Just as your narrative you have invested
    With pathos, or with humour us beguil'd ;
Much of good feeling, too, you've manifested,
    Altho' 'tis true, you've been a little wild ;
Upon the whole, I really quite admire you,
And for a servant ever shall desire you.

CXIV.

" Don't think that I was sleeping. 'Tis my way
    When much amus'd, to keep my eyelids clos'd ;
Take not offence, then, at this habit, pray,
    Nor think a single moment that I doz'd.
But come, let's mix a bumper. All, obey,
    By me a health's about to be propos'd—
Fill, fill, my lads ; demands a parting glass
Old Adam's health—so round the liquor pass."

CXV.

We drank the health, of course, with acclamation.
    Returning thanks, old Adam made a speech,
In which he told us, much in estimation
    He held our kindness, that his heart did reach.
Then having held a little conversation,
    The Major said it would appear a breach
Of manners, should we longer there remain,
And from the ladies' company abstain.

CXVI.

Therefore we join'd our hostess, when we found
  Bill and his lady-love in kindly chat;
While Mrs. Horner, wrapt in slumber sound,
  In an arm-chair most comfortably sat;
Who as we enter'd, gap'd, and look'd around,
  As if in wonder what we could be at.
She rang the bell, and order'd in the tray,
That with a supper we might end the day.

CXVII.

We supp'd—recurring to old Adam's tale
  For our amusement.   To his wife and daughter
The Major did its incidents detail,
  Dwelling with gusto on the scene of slaughter.
Bella did Alice's sad fate bewail;
  And quite deserving our compassion thought her;
While Mrs. Horner said she was a hussey,
" Stuck-up, conceited, impudent, and fussy."

CXVIII.

At last the time for our retiring came,
  And so to each and all we wish'd " good night."
Bill paus'd and sigh'd when he approach'd his flame,
  As if to kiss her would afford delight;
But this he could not do for very shame;
  Therefore in his he grasp'd her fingers tight.
She handed to him promptly a bed-candle,
While standing at the door, I held the handle.

CXIX.

That closing door must part us—envious door!
  My gentle reader, but we meet again;
My rude harp for your ear I'll tune once more,
  And strike upon it a melodious strain.
A door has parted lovers, till the core
  Of each fond heart was breaking—but in vain.
A door must part us, but we soon shall meet,
And a re-union is always sweet.

END OF CANTO VI.

M

CANTO VII.

I.

On, sleep, thou art, indeed, a glorious thing!
   Dreamless, refreshing, care-dispelling sleep;
What pleasure to the weary dost thou bring,
   As on the senses thou dost gently creep.
And e'en if fancy, upon airy wing,
   Should flit o'er scenes constraining one to weep,
Still thou art grateful; and the dawning day
Drives the chimeras with its light away.

II.

Still thou art grateful; for the frame renew'd
   Rises with eagerness to life again;
The dreams are gone—no sorrow has accrued—
   The morning dissipates the fancied pain.
Look from your window on the grass bedew'd
   With pearls no jeweller could e'er obtain;
Gaze on the sky—on that cerulean dome
Hope, life, you find, annihilating gloom.

III.

I slept most soundly, and the morning sun
   Was peeping thro' my curtains ere I rose—
Phœbus his daily journey had begun,
   While still I lay enjoying my repose.
I woke, and listen'd—murmur there was none—
   'Twas yet too early; so again to close
My eyes in slumber I determined till
I should be summon'd from my bed by Bill.

IV.

How long I slept I know not ; but a noise
    Like people scuffling, at my door outside,
Awoke me ; and upspringing I did poise
    Myself on tiptoe, and my eye applied
To the keyhole.—When Duncan in the joys
    Of snatching kisses from his love I spied ;
I must observe she seemed not *too* unwilling,
But with good grace submitted to his billing.

V.

She freed herself at last, and down the stairs
    The twain proceeded—thinking nought of me—
Employ'd them at the time far sweeter cares,
    In which their thoughts did cordially agree.
" 'Tis time to dress," quoth I—" if Bill thus dares,
    Certain of being from interruption free,
To kiss his sweetheart, fearing not the Major,
They are at breakfast, I'll lay any wager."

VI.

Therefore I cloth'd myself with all due speed,
    And to the dining-room in haste descended,
Prepar'd, with rav'nous appetite, to feed
    On whatso'er my hostess recommended.
A breakfast is a *dejéuner* indeed
    In Canada, and not the meal pretended
O'er which the Cockney dallies—tea and toast.
A breakfast, truly !—'tis a breakfast's ghost !

VII.

Breakfast across the Atlantic signifies
    Something substantial—something worth attacking—
Which hungry Yankees fully satisfies,
    And e'en a stranger's lips affects to smacking,
Beefsteaks, veal cutlets, all sorts of meat pies.
    In short, of dinner nothing there is lacking—
With tea and coffee, toast and bread and butter,
Besides huge joints attractive to the cutter.

VIII.

This meal enjoying I found all assembled ;
   The major most voraciously was eating—
Bella, still mindful of the kissing, trembled—
   And Mrs. H. was at the urn, completing
Her matronly arrangements.—Bill dissembled
   The happiness he felt ; and, after greeting
Me, chid me roundly for my late appearance,
To early hours advising strict adherence.

IX.

I well nigh answer'd —" Had I the attraction
   Which drew you from your bed, I'd been a riser
Long before this ;" but seeing a contraction
   Upon his brow, as I commenc'd, a wiser
Course I adopted, lest dissatisfaction
   He should evince, were I the advertiser
Of that love-skirmish, which my keyhole show'd me,
Tho' malice on to mention it did goad me.

X.

And Bella look'd so pretty and so blushing,
   I had been cruel if to her confusion
I'd added—consciousness her face was flushing,
   Which bloom'd all roses in its sweet suffusion—
Her little fingers were employ'd in crushing
   Her sash—'twas clear she dreaded an allusion
To that to which I might have been a witness—
To be retail'd she knew well its unfitness.

XI.

As I regarded her, I did not wonder
   At Bill, unable to resist temptation,
Kissing her lips—altho' he made a blunder
   In doing so within my observation.
Her dress was white, and where its folds asunder
   Just shew'd her bosom's gentle undulation,
A muslin front, worked exquisitely, tried
To add to charms its drap'ry could not hide.

XII.

Health glow'd upon her cheek, and in her eyes
    Love beam'd—but maiden love—no wild desire
Did from those deep blue orbs impetuous rise,
    Shocking the gazer with immodest fire.
She was all innocence, and *this* supplies
    E'en lack of beauty—*this* all *must* admire :
When first I saw her she appeared most charming,
But *now* her loveliness was quite alarming.

XIII.

My heart was gone, or she had ta'en possession
    Of that which is inflammable—in sooth.
I have been constant, so may make confession
    Of my susceptibility in youth.
Bella produced upon me an impression
    Which made me feel—I dare not tell the truth—
But I began to look at Bill morosely,
As, toying, to his love he press'd more closely

XIV.

Breakfast's a cosy meal—or should be so,
    A meal to linger o'er in friendly chat ;
Such was the one we took—its process slow
    As the arrangement of a white cravat.
Bill knew at night he'd promised me to go,
    Therefore with Bella he conversing sat,
Making the most of time, which will not stay
For lover's pray'r, but sternly glides away.

XV.

At last, however, satisfied, we rose,
    The ladies to their household cares withdrew ;
Bill took the Major with him to propose
    For Bella—which the latter doubtless knew
Was his intention, so did not oppose
    My friend's desire strong for an interview ;
Then was I left alone—a situation
Adapted well to serious cogitation.

XVI.

I had not tarried long in solitude,
 When me arous'd a rapping at the door ;
And soon I heard a voice, in accents rude,
 Demanding instant entrance ; and before
I could arrange my thoughts, there did intrude,
 By " Blackey " led, a form I'd seen of yore—
I bow'd politely—a reception cool
To the new-comer giving—'twas O'Toole.

XVII.

I will describe his dress : a coat of grey—
 Such as the *habitans* delight to wear
In Lower Canada—him did betray
 To have resided in the country there—
His nether limbs, with many a stain of clay
 Discolor'd, were defended by a pair
Of trousers of the same cloth as his coat ;
And both contempt for smartness did denote.

XVIII.

A small glaz'd hat was jauntily applied
 To his round bullet head, whereon it hung
So insecurely plac'd, that had I tried,
 With gentle push, it on the ground I'd flung—
His shoes, in which, with a gigantic stride,
 O'Toole, when put in motion, active sprung,
Like those were French Canadians on the turf
Press as they walk, call'd *Souliers de bœuf.*

XIX.

His face was pale and bloated—red his nose,
 And his eyes twinkled with a roguish fire—
Six feet in height from mother Earth he rose,
 And being thin, his stature seem'd still higher ;
A large knobb'd stick his fingers did enclose.
 His morning's walk had caus'd him to perspire,
When he broke on me musing. Having caught
A glimpse of me, he vanish'd quick as thought.

XX.

The house he quitted, and, with rapid pace,
　　I saw him striding towards the entrance gate ;
Glad to be rid of him, I gave no chase,
　　For once it had been my unlucky fate
To bring upon him merited disgrace—
　　I will the story to your ear relate,
While Bill with Major Horner is discussing
What is to be the upshot of his bussing.

XXI.

" When I arriv'd in Canada, at first
　　My knowledge of the language was but slight —
I mean the French ;—and therefore to be vers'd
　　In it my anxious wish was, that I might
Talk glibly with the *habitans*, dispers'd
　　Over the country.　As I took delight
In wand'ring—French was absolutely needful,
And so to learn it early I was heedful.

XXII.

" When I reach'd Montreal, I look'd about
　　For lodgings in the country where they spoke
Nothing but French ; that being so, without
　　Means of conversing, did I not invoke
Those I was talking with the day throughout
　　In the same language, which from their lips broke,
Of it I must learn something. e'en if stupid—
To speak it well I manag'd, thanks to Cupid.

XXIII.

" I found the spot I needed, not far distant—
　　My host, a one-ey'd man, the village notary,
Was glad of me to act as his assistant,
　　While to acquire his tongue I was a votary ;
My board I paid for, which was inconsistent,
　　Seeing I work'd hard when I join'd his coterie—
But as the work increas'd my Gallic knowledge,
I did it freely, unlike youths at college.

XXIV.

" The family consisted of mine host,
 His wife, and cousin, who was very pretty—
Indeed, in England she'd have been a ' toast,'
 With her black sparkling eyes and ringlets jetty—
I mean the cousin, for the wife could boast
 No charms—a lodger whose sirname was Getty,
The notary's mother, and his children twain,
Of whom he was preposterously vain.

XXV.

" 'Twas here I met O'Toole, who then was living
 With *Léonard,* the notary I have named ;
He caus'd me much annoy, which I forgiving,
 Because his mind unhappily was fram'd—
Falsely that I was cowardly conceiving
 To bully me he did not feel ashamed—
I prov'd myself, however, in the sequel,
To stopping his impertinence quite equal.

XXVI.

" He'd been a soldier, and was made the butt
 Of all the mess with which he was connected ;
Who jokes more practical than pleasant put
 Upon him, made by this means disaffected—
By the more gentlemanly he was cut,
 Which soured his temper much when he reflected—
In fact the army quite a purgatory
Became to him, who had no thirst for glory.

XXVII.

" One night the officers had drank much wine,
 O'Toole had taken also his full share ;
When to retire to rest he did incline,
 And so to bed in good time did repair—
His brother officers of his design
 And its fulfilment perfectly aware,
Determin'd to disturb him while reposing,
And drag him from where he was snugly dozing.

XXVIII.

" It was in winter, and the nights were cold,
    Which most unpleasant made the operation
Of being imbedded, when compactly rolled
    Between the sheets, in dreamy contemplation.
The mess together did joint counsel hold—
    Then at O'Toole's room-door they took their station ;
Which finding lock'd, they open'd by main force,
And dragg'd him from his bed without remorse.

XXIX.

" Of course at this he was exasperated,
    And struggled wildly—but 'twas all in vain.
They who his sleeping-room had penetrated,
    Were all regardless that he did complain—
Shivering upon the floor they left him, sated
    With their mad frolic, and to wine again
Betook themselves—the while their victim swore
He'd shoot the next who came inside his door.

XXX.

" A short time they carous'd ; and when they thought
    O'Toole to sleep had comfortably sunk,
Fresh madness from their wine cups having caught,
    And some being drunk—some very nearly drunk—
Setting his threat of shooting down as nought
    But idle passion (or they would have shrunk
From acting as they did), to gain his chamber
Once more upstairs they did uproarious clamber.

XXXI.

" O'Toole his door had barricaded since
    Their former visit, and was now prepar'd
To stand a siege—so when did him convince
    The sound without to come again they'd dar'd,
Aloud he shouted—' Devils ! I'll not mince
    The matter, but proceed as I declar'd
When you came here before,'—I have my gun,
And I will shoot you if you do not run.

XXXII.

" Of this they took no notice, but procur'd,
    Of which they made a battering ram, a form--
The captain told the rest he was assur'd
    They would not meet with a reception warm ;
And so themselves from injury secur'd
    Thinking, they went to work the room to storm
With their strange instrument of warfare, each
Straining his muscles to effect a breach.

XXXIII.

" This they soon did ; for off its hinges flew
    The door, and so an entrance-way was clear'd—
But now O'Toole convinc'd them it was true
    About the gun—for ere the bed they near'd
He fir'd—that shot a young lieutenant slew,
    Who to aggression had most loudly cheer'd,
And was the foremost to approach the bed,
On which he fell beside his slayer—dead.

XXXIV.

" This sobered the whole party.   They retir'd
    A moment, then return'd too seek their friend—
O'Toole declar'd he knew not, when he fir'd,
    The gun was loaded.   An untimely end
Thus found a gay young man by all admir'd.
    In an adjoining room they did extend
His corpse, and sought their beds, but could not sleep.
Their sorrow for their frolic was too deep.

XXXV.

" Of course there was inquiry, and to quit
    The service he who'd fired was compell'd ;
He for an officer had ne'er been fit,
    And thus was from its ranks almost expell'd
By a court martial, which on him did sit—
    Half-pay, however, had not been withheld—
The court *advis'd* immediate retirement,
O'Toole, at once, complied with its requirement.

XXXVI.

" I found him at my lodging, at Ste. Rose,
    Where, with an iron hand, he rul'd supreme—
The notary did not dare his will oppose.
    The females had of him a fear extreme.
Grown angry, all around him he thought foes,
    So that insane you oft-times would him deem—
He was most courteous for some time to me,
Therefore, at first, we manag'd to agree.

XXXVII.

" We scour'd the country in pursuit of game
    ('Twas winter then, and cover'd was the ground
With snow), and almost friendly we became,
    In these our rambles in the woodland round.
An old French *habitant* of sinewy frame,
    Much entertainment walking with us found—
We call'd him *Fanfan,* an odd *nom de guerre*
For an old fellow rough as any bear.

XXXVIII.

" Snow-birds and hares we usually shot,
    Which were converted into soups and pies ;
The latter animals resemble not
    The English hare, being smaller far in size—
White are they, too, with here and there a spot
    Of russet fur upon their backs and thighs—
So it requires considerable skill   ·
In shooting, in the snow, poor puss to kill.

XXXIX.

" Old *Fanfan* was a curious specimen
    Of the Canadian peasant.   Not a care
Disturb'd his heart ; most free from guile of men,
    His sirname did his character declare—
Sans Souci was he hight, and to his ken
    All troubles seem'd like trifles " light as air."
He had two grown-up sons and two sweet daughters,
With voices musical as rippling waters.

XL.

" *Marie Ma belle Marie—Ma petite femme!*
 (For so I us'd to call you in those days)—
Older and wiser now perhaps I am—
 But still upon me did your black eyes blaze ;
And romp'd you with me, playful as a lamb—
 I am afraid again my boyish ways
Would all resume their power—I'd snatch a kiss
From those sweet ruby lips which pouted bliss.

XLI.

" What jokes we crack'd together !—What delight
 It was, as gathering round that rude old stove
Within your father's cabin, the long night
 We spent in prattling joyously of love ;
No passion did, 'tis true, our hearts affright—
 Jocund we were, and graceful as a dove
You flutter'd near me—oh ! my aching heart
Much changed since then—much changed indeed thou art.

XLII.

" Years have roll'd o'er me.   Old before my time,
 I cling to the illusions of the past —
Of age e'en now I have not reached my prime,
 But all my youthful dreams are fading fast.
Oh ! for the bright days of that genial clime—
 Genial, tho' cold—oh ! for the forest vast—
The sparkling rivers—freedom unrestrain'd—
Amongst the crowd of men what have I gained ?

XLIII.

" I have gain'd nothing—I have lost my all,
 That freshness of the heart, the sole true joy—
Pleasure were sweet, if it did never pall,
 And worldly wealth, if care did ne'er annoy.
My lot has been on bitterness to fall—
 Oh ! that I were again that wand'ring boy !
Marie ! Ma belle Marie !—Ma petite femme !
From what I was with you how changed I am.

XLIV.

" Where was I ? Oh, with my friend *Sans Souci,*
　　Before his daughter on my mem'ry flash'd,
With her sweet smile and winning courtesy,
　　Not shrinking, like an English girl, abash'd ;
But unconstrain'd in manner all and free,
　　Tho' no immodesty her conduct dash'd ;
She was a lovely little maid, in sooth,
Blooming with health, and radiant with youth.

XLV.

" Well, on a morning, while still in my bed,
　　As the last dosing minutes I did pass,
Approach'd my chamber door the heavy tread
　　Of old *Fanfan* (if there were not a mass),
And tapping, in loud tones, the ancient said,
　　Il fait beau temps pour aller à la chasse
Debout ! Monsieur, il ne faut pas attendre
Debout ! Je vais les lièvres surprendre.

XLVI.

" And then I us'd to rise and don my clothes,
　　Calling O'Toole, whose chamber join'd my own,
And after breakfast, out upon the snows,
　　To which by this time I'd accustom'd grown
Shooting we went, without a dog to nose
　　Our game, which from him would have fled or flown—
Because in winter there no scent will lie,
So that to *find,* we trusted to the eye.

XLVII.

" The snow, like dry salt, crumbled 'neath our feet,
　　And our cheeks tingled with the biting wind ;
And tho' with fur our garments were complete,
　　Intensely cutting we the air did find,
Till warm'd by exercise ; when quite a treat
　　We thought the bracing atmosphere, combined
With the blue sky and ever-shining sun—
The day a contrast to an English one.

XLVIII.

" E'en mighty forest trees the frost would split—
　　I've heard their cracking like the cannon's roar ;
I fear'd they'd fall and crush us—not a whit
　　Of apprehension, striding on-before,
Of this had *Fanfan*—he would pause a bit
　　As I exclaim'd, and his grim face came o'er
A pitying smile—he knew there was no danger,
As in the woods for years he'd been a ranger.

XLIX.

" An old flint gun he had, which oft miss'd fire,
　　A curious weapon. but a weapon still—
It had descended from his great grandsire
　　With a small farm 'twas *Fanfan's* care to till ;
With this he popp'd away, until did tire
　　His patience the vile tube which would *not* kill—
Our English fire-arms he'd then gladly borrow,
His own regarding with a comic sorrow.

L.

" And so we laugh'd and chatted thro' the day,
　　Returning to our home as evening clos'd,
When on the table viands to allay
　　Our hunger smoked. As we had been expos'd
For weary hours to cold intense you may
　　Imagine with the food we promptly closed—
While Zoe gladly ev'ry want supplied.
To wait upon us was with her a pride.

LI.

" ' And who was Zoe ? What a pretty name !'
　　I think I hear my very reader cry—
She was the notary's cousin, and my flame,
　　While he a lodging to me did supply ;
She was a glorious creature, and to frame
　　French phrases she to teach my lips did try ;
We talked of love, and, after many a blunder,
My progress in the language was a wonder.

LII.

" I'll sketch her. Glossy locks of raven hue
  Down on her snowy shoulders wanton hung,
Veiling a little from your amorous view
  The rosy cheeks, to which they sometimes clung
Like tendrils of the vine, and then anew
  Were by the breeze in motion loosely flung ;
Her nose was small and straight, her lips within—
How white her teeth !—how beautiful her chin !

LIII.

" And then her eye ! her deep black dreamy eye,
  Now soft with love, and now with angry glare
Gleaming upon you, as if 'twere to try
  If you an insult or a slight would dare—
Then with mirth flashing, seeming to defy
  It to suffuse the most heart-rending care ;
A pensive glance would then assume that orb,
Giv'n to smite, to madden, to absorb.

LIV.

" Her form was tall and exquisitely slight,
  Yet rounded well in a luxuriant mould.
Her every motion gave the eye delight;
  And when this arm such loveliness did hold,
(This arm now doom'd of it to merely write)
  While down the dance in frolic uncontroll'd
We whisk'd, I thought, and you would, had you seen us,
Have also thought her a Canadian Venus.

LV,

" She liked me—Did that liking turn to love ?
  I knew not then, and now shall never know—
Perhaps to it I'd had the pow'r to move
  Her bosom, had I wish'd it to be so ;
But my young heart was free as air—nor strove
  With passion's fire to make that sweet one glow—
When in the house I was by stress of weather
Kept,—oh ! what happy days we pass'd together.

LVI.

" She taught me to speak French ; and gratitude
   For that instruction led me to present
Her with a torquoise ring, which, when she view'd,
   Upon my shoulder girlishly she leant,
And to my lips her own, impulsive, glued ;
   Oh ! what a thrill thro' all my members sent
That kiss the honey lingers to this day—
I taste it now, tho' years have roll'd away.

LVII.

" Oh ! Zoe, had I lov'd thee—my sad fate
   Might not have come upon me, and with thee
In some secluded spot for my helpmate,
   By all the world forgotten, joyous, free—
With nought but pleasure to anticipate,
   And nought but happiness around to see,
I might have liv'd—had I with accent low
But whisper'd ' Ζωη μου, σας αγαπω.'

LVIII.

" To drive about I bought a horse and sleigh—
   Sleighing's indeed delightful locomotion—
Down the St. Lawrence I my watery way
   Have held—and 'mid the billows of the ocean
I have been rock'd, to howling winds a prey,
   So that the tars betook them to devotion—
My feelings were sublime, but tame and vapid
To those which gives the sleigh's progression rapid.

LIX.

" Ha ! it is glorious on the harden'd snow
   Smoothly to glide, the while the tinkling bells
In the clear air make music as you go
   To your steeds' motions ; on the ear it swells
With varying cadence, mournful now as slow
   You move—then swifter action loudly tells
Upon the tiny instruments whose sound
With a heart glad'ning tone to ring is found.

LX.

" My mare was of the true Canadian breed,
    Hardy and swift—her colour almost white ;
Of whip to urge her I had never need.
    She trotted on as if extreme delight
It gave her o'er the frozen snow to speed ;
    While the bells' silvery tinkling to her flight
Made music—and behind all wrapp'd in fur,
Within the sleigh I sat admiring her.

LXI.

" With Zoe and the notary's wife I'd drive
    To visit all their neighbours. 'Tis a season,
Christmas, in Canada, when priests do shrive
    Their flocks ; who then considering they have reason,
After their sins are all wip'd out, contrive
    To feast them, thinking it to heaven no treason.
And so they dance and sing, and in flirtation
The girls engage with wondrous animation.

LXII.

" A short time after Christmas, Zoe quitted
    The notary's house, returning to her home ;
Where as a guest I often was admitted,
    For a great favourite I was become
With all her friends, who jokingly me twitted
    About my *penchant* for her—indeed some
Thought that my feelings on that score were ' *tendre*,'
And her papa address'd me as ' *son gendre*.'

LXIII.

" But Zoe knew full well I'd never utter'd
    A word of love ; tho' often admiration
I had express'd, which not a little flutter'd
    Her, as together we held conversation—
When I paid compliments, she paus'd and stutter'd
    In her replies—which made my situation
Embarrassing, and as I much respected her,
I ceas'd from using phrases that affected her.

N

LXIV.

" And so we grew more distant towards each other ;
    I found new friends, and therefore did not see
So much of her—I lov'd her as a brother,
    Was it a sister's love she bore to me ?
I doubt it was not ! Soon I found another,
    Who charm'd my fancy, of my own degree.
Zoe I never, never could have married—
'Twas better she no longer with us tarried.

LXV.

" There was a seigneur lived near Ste. Thérese.
    The house stood by a swiftly rolling stream,
Where in the limpid waters you may gaze,
    As I have oft done, and in gazing, dream.
What airy castles on its banks to raise
    Did I contrive, which now all baseless seem—
Yet they were goodly structures. The ideal
Is so superior to the sober real.

LXVI.

" One evening I was driving past his house—
    I now forget precisely where I'd been—
When something suddenly my mare did rouse,
    Something her musing master had not seen—
Whether some bird in motion, on the boughs
    Of the adjoining trees awoke her spleen
I know not—but she wildly leap'd aside
Ere her first irritation I descried.

LXVII.

" I saw no more—I heard a startling crash,
    And felt that I was whirl'd from off my seat.
Before my eyes a sort of mazy flash
    Glanc'd for a moment. Then my temple beat
Against the hard snow, with a frightful dash ;
    And loss of animation was complete.
Thus stunn'd and motionless sometime I lay,
My chance but small to see another day.

LXVIII.

" I woke to life, to consciousness, to bliss—
    A lovely face in scrutiny was bending
Over my bleeding brow.   I long'd to kiss
    The lips whose breathing with my own was blending—
A country girl stood near, preventing this,
    Her mistress in her charity attending—
Half-fainting as I lay that vision fair
Led me to think it was an angel there.

LXIX.

" She bath'd my wound—so tender was the touch
    Her ivory fingers laid upon the sore ;
Her pitying smile so sweet, the kindness such
    Which her expression towards the sufferer bore,
I felt enchanted, for the joy was much,
    Much greater than the pain that me came o'er ;
She took my hand her fairy hands between,
And felt my pulse—*Ma charmante Caroline.*

LXX.

" Oh ! it were pleasure, long, long years to lie,
    As then I did, with such a doctor near,
To catch assidious the gasping sigh,
    And to the moans of pain to lend an ear ;
What salve so healing as that love-fraught eye,
    In which compassion form'd an embryo tear !—
Thou wert indeed a talisman to cure !
My own sweet Caroline—so bright, so pure.

LXXI.

" She bound my brow, and gave me wine and water,
    Then left me on the sofa to recover
My scatter'd senses—that old seigneur's daughter—
    Perhaps not dreaming she had gain'd a lover—
Her training in a nunnery had taught her
    The art in dressing wounds she did discover.
Far better had it been for her—for me
Had I that sweet face never chanc'd to see.

LXXII.

"Some time confus'd I lay—then sleep came o'er me,
   A troubled sleep, which held my senses long,
And when I woke, standing I found before me,
   A fine old man of sinewy frame and strong,
The sire of her who'd labour'd to restore me,
   Nature, her nobles him had plac'd among—
His high receding forehead, speaking eye,
Betoken'd intellect within did lie.

LXXIII.

"He spoke to me (his accent was so pure,
   I ne'er heard French from manly lips like his),
Asking if he could for me aught procure,
   And how I felt myself?—'Not much amiss,'
I made response—'I could a wound endure
   Ten times more grievous in its pain than this,
Did you, monsieur, such lovely surgeons find
As her whose lily hands my brow did bind.'

LXXIV.

"He smil'd (the compliment had power to charm),
   And ask'd me would I wish to see my nurse?
'Most certainly,' I answered, growing warm
   And starting suddenly, which made me worse.
I sank back almost fainting. In alarm
   At his imprudence, which had the reverse
Effect on me to that which he'd intended,
The old man 'neath my head his arm extended,

LXXV.

"And sprinkl'd water on my face—the shower
   Recall'd me to myself, but still the pain
Was exquisite; for nearly half-an-hour
   Me on his arm the seigneur did retain,
Using all means which lay within his pow'r
   That I might not to faintness sink again.
No father o'er his only son could dwell
More kindly than o'er me did *Lachapelle*.

LXXVI.

" His daughter joined us while he held me there,
    And with her came young Lachapelle her brother—
She said my bedroom they did then prepare,
    The servant-maids, assisted by her mother,
Who had been absent when to stranger's care
    My fate had me consign'd, deprived of other—
Soon the old lady enter'd and assur'd me
A comfortable bed she had secured me.

LXXVII.

" I wish'd my nurse 'good night ;' and son and sire
    My tottering steps supported to my bed—
Within a stove there burn'd a cheerful fire,
    Which genial warmth around the chamber spread.
In bed they plac'd me, then did both retire,
    As on the pillow I repos'd my head—
Pain made me restless for a time, but sleep
At last upon my weary eyes did creep.

LXXVIII.

" The morning found me better, but for days
    I could not leave my rooms ; the surgeon came,
And much my lovely doctor's skill did praise,
    As who, indeed, so sweet an one could blame !
And when at last my wounded head to raise
    And leave my bed, me ready did proclaim
My medical adviser, thy sweet smile,
My love, was prompt, my sufferings to beguile.

LXXIX.

" My days of convalescence, oh ! how sweet
    That happy period of my chequer'd life—
Each morning, Caroline, thine eye did greet
    Thy patient, who, tho' still with suff'ring rife,
Felt that on earth no pleasure could compete
    With pain that made him woo thee for his wife—
Thine eye did greet him, with its kindly beam,
That eye itself was pure affection's dream.

LXXX.

" We spent our time together, and she sang,
   That angel girl, she sang to the guitar—
With her melodious voice th' apartment rang,
   Full in its compass, and the sweetest far
I ever heard—upon my couch she'd hang
   (For none there was our growing love to mar)
And trill her French songs with such witching pow'r,
That every cadence did my heart devour.

LXXXI.

" And so from day to day we fonder grew.
   We never mentioned love, but felt its force ;
Her eye spoke volumes in its depths of blue,
   And mine responded to that glance, of course,
And I would gaze upon her till the hue
   In her bright cheek was deepened from the source —
Whence sprang that tell-tale crimson her pure heart
Which, conscious, did that radiant current start.

LXXXII.

" When health return'd, reluctantly I went—
   Went to my lodgings at the notary's back—
A deeper wound within my bosom pent
   Than that which lately had been heal'd, alack !
Then to my feelings I did give no vent,
   Tho' silence kept my heart upon the rack
Of doubt—I trusted to a future day,
While hope assur'd me with its cheering ray.

LXXXIII.

" I found O'Toole more troublesome than ever—
   A week I stood his nonsense ; then, one night,
After he'd bullied me, a lesson, never
   By him forgotten, but deserved quite,
I gave, which did our intimacy sever,
   And caus'd the fellow a tremendous fright—
I wrote a challenge, sent it in a letter
By a young doctor, who was my abettor.

LXXXIV.

" He would not fight, declaring he was drunk
　　When he insulted me, and so declin'd ;
The matter gave him such a glorious funk,
　　And acted so much on his cowardly mind,
That from the notary's away he slunk,
　　And his apartment there at once resign'd—
So never more again, thank heav'n, I saw him,
Till when he did so speedily withdraw him.

LXXXV.

" When I left Monsieur Lachapelle's he gave
　　Me to revisit him an invitation—
And you I tell no liberated slave,
　　Upon the morn of his emancipation,
Having the boon that he so long did crave,
　　E'er felt that I did half the exultation—
When forth I sallied one fine clear March morning,
Tow'rd Sainte Therese, the bitter weather scorning.

LXXXVI.

" I was on foot, and the cold bracing air
　　Felt not unpleasant, for with exercise
I soon was in a glow ; my only care
　　A means to tell my passion to devise.
I knew I had no reason to despair,
　　Or falsehoods me had told my charmer's eyes—
And so as I approach'd the seigneur's dwelling,
With hopes of happiness my heart was swelling.

LXXXVII.

" Monsieur and Madame Lachapelle were out—
　　Were gone to Montreal to spend the day,
So that of my success I did not doubt,
　　If but the brother I could draw away ;
When I met Caroline, a pretty pout
　　Her lips assum'd—' Where have you been, sir, pray ?
I thought you had forgotten me !' she cried—
' To have done that,' I said, ' I must have died !'

LXXXVIII.

" And so we fell into a cosy chat—
    She look'd so lovely I felt quite exstatic ;
Indeed scarce knowing what I would be at,
    Or whether 'twas the parlour or the attic
In which absorb'd in loving talk we sat.
    My worship of that girl became fanatic—
And now it is my creed, I do declare,
That angels all have blue eyes and black hair.

LXXXIX.

" We din'd—her brother saw he was *de trôp*,
    And left us with true French consideration ;
Now, thought I, this is very *ápropos*,
    While my heart beat with nervous palpitation ;
But Caroline's fair cheek did brighter glow,
    And her eyes sparkled with more animation—
Her woman's heart prophetic warning gave
That I should soon profess myself her slave.

XC.

" Her heart was right ; I rose, and on her chair
    Leant till my lips well-nigh in contact came
With that small waxen ear, which to her hair
    Contrasted so, and did the lily shame ;
And with face flushed, and eyes all melting, there,
    Love prompting words, I told my hidden flame ;
She made no answer, but her hand presented,
I took it in my own—her squeeze consented.

XCI.

" And then upon her lips a burning kiss,
    While my arm circling on her ivory shoulder
Rested—I press'd, and linger'd there in bliss.
    My young heart, by her willingness, grown bolder,
To repetition prompted me of this—
    Unconscious that upon us a beholder
Was all the time, thro' the half open door,
Gazing, as I my feelings forth did pour.

XCII.

" At last we ceased from kissing, calmer grown,
    And, seated side by side, our plans discuss'd—
To Monsieur Lachapelle, her sire, make known,
    Of course, th' engagement I had form'd, I must ;
And Caroline was certain that her own
    Choice would be his, and I in her did trust ;
So that we thought our happiness complete—
Alas ! 'twas all delusion, but how sweet.

XCIII.

" The serpent was already nigh at hand,
    With venom flush'd, preparing for his spring ;
A young priest, list'ning to our words, did stand,
    Determin'd, though our fond hearts he should wring,
To frustrate all the happiness we'd plann'd—
    That reptile priest, how baneful was his sting !
I turn'd, and then observ'd the door ajar,
Not thinking one stood there our hopes to mar.

XCIV.

" I clos'd it ; at the time not taking heed
    Of the retreating footsteps, whose faint sound
Fell on my ear, as he away did speed,
    Whose hate so deadly afterwards I found.
I thought some servant-girl did then proceed
    Across the hall, and therefore looked not round ;
But I remember'd, when 'twas all too late,
The circumstance decisive of my fate.

XCV.

" Young Lachapelle return'd, a stranger brought,
    In priestly garments, whom he introduc'd
As his own cousin—and the man methought
    Look'd scowling on me. This might have induc'd
A settled gloom from his vocation caught,
    Which might in him have bigotry produc'd ;
I therefore notic'd little his black brow,
Which did, howe'er, disquietude avow.

XCVI.

" I did observe, though, that to Caroline
    He acted more the lover than the priest ;
In truth, his manner somewhat rais'd my spleen —
    Upon her face his piercing eyes did feast —
And there was something devilish in his mien,
    Mocking and sensual.   He from gazing ceas'd
At last, and joining in our conversation,
He question'd me about the English nation.

XCVII.

" We chatted sociably, until arriv'd
    Monsieur and Madame Lachapelle, whose greeting
Of me was kindly—of all form depriv'd—
    In sooth it was a very happy meeting.
To pass a pleasant evening we contriv'd,
    And to Monsieur I spoke, his ear entreating ·
To listen, in the morning, to my love tale,
Hoping his views would with my wishes dove-tail.

XCVIII.

" The morning came—I saw old Lachapelle,
    And told him what had pass'd the previous day ;
He said that Caroline had chosen well,
    And hoped she would my love for her repay.
He only wished that near him we might dwell,
    And pressed me much in Canada to stay—
To this I did not make the least objection,
The seigneur's project thinking quite perfection.

XCIX.

" And so we were betrothed, my nurse and I,
    And many happy days we spent together—
I left her then—but to her still would hie,
    As spring advanc'd, and warmer grew the weather,
To visit her—departing with a sigh—
    (Alas ! we sigh so often in this nether
World, where the smile is follow'd by the tear !)
Thus pass'd our time till summer did appear.

C.

" I then went on a tour.   The Northern States
    I visited, enjoining Caroline
To write to me at Boston, where the Fates
    Ordain'd, when I had there a short time been,
That I should meet one of my old school-mates,
    Employ'd, observing all things to be seen
On Yankee ground ; by whose wish I agreed
To Maine and Vermont with him to proceed.

CI.

" At Boston I receiv'd the only letter
    Which Caroline to me did ever write—
She was quite well—never, indeed, was better,
    And look'd for my return with much delight ;
I wrote, describing with how much regret her
    Dear self, I must, in absence, day and night,
Still see in my imagination only,
And saying that this thought made me feel lonely.

CII.

" I told her also that she must address
    To Burlington what letters she might send,
Where I should soon be ; and what happiness
    It gave me reading that which she had penn'd ;
A month elaps'd—it might be more or less—
    When to Vermont we went, myself and friend—
At Burlington a week or more we stay'd—
No letter came—at this I felt dismay'd.

CIII.

" But my companion laugh'd away my fears ;
    And so I wrote—another town assign'd
To Caroline.   Where hill on hill appears,
    We wander'd then for weeks—an undefin'd
Dread of misfortune, which in after years
    I oft have felt, would pray upon my mind—
Altho' 'midst Nature's beauties I *seem'd* glad,
'Twas but a semblance—for I felt most sad.

CIV.

" Still came no letter ; urgent business call'd
    Me down to Portland in the State of Maine—
No letter still   I was, indeed, appall'd,
    And wrote to Caroline again, again ;
Dejected, to the post-office I crawl'd
    Day after day—inquiries there were vain—
'Twas winter now, and, fast as steeds could fly,
Towards Montreal I did, despondent, hie.

CV.

" I slept not on the way—scarce tasted food,
    So that, when I alighted, of repose
I had great need—but in no resting mood,
    From Montreal even to my journey's close
I travell'd on—the while my mind did brood
    Over my love's strange silence.   From a doze
I started as we enter'd Sainte Therese,
And thought with pain on former happy days.

CVI.

" Of Caroline reminded me each tree—
    Along *that* path we lovingly had stray'd—
Upon *this* bank she had repos'd with me,
    And we had paus'd together in *that* glade ;
Oh ! it was agony around to see
    All Nature eloquent of that sweet maid !
My heart was breaking when I reach'd the door,
Where we had parted six short months before.

CVII.

" I knock'd—the servant came,—but with affright
    She started when she saw me—in low tones
I ask'd for Caroline ; and tow'rds the light,
    Which from the parlour stream'd (the while with groans
I fill'd the air) I hasted in in spite
    Of her who would have stopp'd me ; for the moans
To which my voice had sunk, had made her dread
That I with madness was disquieted.

CVIII.

" I reach'd the room—Monsieur alone was there—
Him I approach'd, but with averted eye
He turned away—in accents of despair
    I ask'd for Caroline—but no reply ;
At length I said more calmly, ' this affair
    ⸝ Needs explanation—tell me—tell me why
You do not welcome me, my almost father ?
Something is wrong, but what I cannot gather.'

CIX.

" He look'd upon me with a mournful gaze,
    And said, ' Monsieur, your manner makes me fear
We have been much misled : not many days
    After you left us Belanger was here ;
He told us that which fill'd us with amaze,
    And produc'd letters from which it seem'd clear
That you, my destin'd son-in-law (I can
Scarcely express it), were a married man.'

CX.

" ' Married !' I cried—' and what said Caroline ? '
    ' She pin'd away for weeks, and scarcely spoke,
But wander'd daily where with you she'd been—
    Her mind was shatter'd by the fatal stroke
Which her and happiness had come between ;
    One summer morning from the house she broke
Before we rose— upon the river's bank
We found her corpse, her clothes and tresses dank.'

CXI.

' ' What, dead ! my darling—said you she was dead ?'
    ' Alas !' he answer'd—but I heard no more ;
' Dead ! dead !' I mutter'd, that pure spirit fled !
    And sank almost as lifeless on the floor.
Weeks after this again I kept my bed
    At the old seigneur's where I lay before—
A fever nearly made me find a grave
Near her whom gladly I'd have died to save.'

END OF CANTO VII.

CANTO VIII.

—

I.

GENTLY she tapp'd my shoulder, as I gaz'd
    Forth from the window, thinking o'er the past ;
I turn'd upon her suddenly, amaz'd,
    For with deep gloom my mind was overcast—
Twas Bella, who, with finger archly rais'd,
    Said, " what, you really *are* awake at last ?
Are you in love, or stupid, that you stand,
Looking as if you self-destruction plann'd ?"

II.

" In love, I answer'd, certainly, *with you*,
    Tho' much I fear mine is a hopeless case—
Nay, do not frown, the thing will never do,
    It mars the loveliness of that sweet face ;
You are engag'd, I know—now don't say, ' pooh !'
    Fibs would those beauteous lips of yours disgrace—
I am in love, I tell you, in despair.
Well may my brow assume a look of care."

III.

And then she laugh'd—how joyous was the ring
    Of Bella's laughter !—it was a mistake
For her mamma, her daughter thus to fling
    Unguarded in my way—was Bill awake ?
Did he suppose I could so fondly cling
    To absent charms as not the most to make
Of such a chance—deem'd he his friend a Scipio ?
Methought what trouble may not to this trip I owe.

IV.

I was in love, but still I had my eyes—
    The poets say, indeed, that love is blind ;
Not that opinions such as theirs I prize,
    For very often strange ideas I find
Set forth by bards, and I will not disguise
    That this one false appears to my poor mind.
Love is all eyes, all ears, how soon you touch
A lover's feelings—blind ! He sees too much.

V.

I thought of Harriet, then at Bella glanc'd,
    Would they were both in one I half exclaim'd—
I grew quite fidgety as time advanc'd,
    And more and more Bill's heedlessness I blam'd :
I talk'd at random, and, I fear, romanc'd,
    Of what I said then, now I feel asham'd—
But really my position quite alarm'd me,
Harriet I wildly lov'd, yet Bella charmed me.

VI.

At last Bill came—he wore a smile of pleasure.
    "Thank Heav'n for this, I now shall be reliev'd"
Methought. He came to take again his treasure,
    Who him with every sign of joy received ;
And now I was compell'd t' employ my leisure
    On other objects, and like one repriev'd
I felt ; for from temptation I could flee,
And no Saint Anthony I claim to be.

VII.

I left the pair, and soon I found mine host,
    With whom to spend the morning I contriv'd ;
We saunter'd round his farm, which was his boast.
    Of other occupation being depriv'd,
Of this 'twas natural he should make the most,
    And show his fields to all who there arriv'd.
He talk'd most learnedly of crops and cattle,
Which now he lov'd as dearly as a battle.

VIII.

We reach'd the house in ample time to dress
 (That is the Major did, I had no change)
For dinner—I was hungry, I confess,
 As o'er the clearing we did widely range
That morning, much, alas ! to my distress,
 Whose mind was occupied by conflicts strange.
I long'd for solitude, and glad, indeed,
I was when from my entertainer freed.

IX.

Within my chamber, all alone, I mus'd
 Upon the past, the present—did I love ?
My conscience for my feelings me accus'd,
 To combat which most earnestly I strove—
Bella ! why was it that thy form refus'd
 To vanish from before me ?—Should I prove
Inconstant, smitten by the first bright eye
Which struck me when my Harriet was not nigh.

X.

Had all my love been spent on Caroline,
 And could affection, worthy of the name,
No more be kindled as it once had been—
 Was all I felt a transitory flame,
By the first fair girl lighted I had seen,
 T' expire as quickly, leaving me the same
Heart-broken, lone, despondent, wayward boy
I was e'er Harriet did my thoughts employ.

XI.

I could not answer this, I was in doubt—
 My heart was form'd for love, for love it crav'd—
But had it found the one by whom without
 Shadow of changing it might be enslav'd ?
" I thought so—but my faith is less devout
 Now, for a trial it has hardly brav'd,"
Said I, soliloquising—" what must be, must be,
I'll trust that chance may well decide for me."

XII.

This was, in point of fact, the sole decision
　　At which I could, with doubt oppress'd, arrive ;
I was uneasy at my strange position,
　　And to be certain of myself did strive.
Rather than live in doubt, were doubt Elysian
　　I'd pray for *certain* misery to deprive
Me of a blessing *certainty* without—
To my mind nought's so wretched as to doubt.

XIII.

Temptation to resist my heart I steel'd,
　　And then descended to the drawing-room,
Fearing, lest to my weakness I should yield,
　　When I should Bella meet in all her bloom
Of beauty, which resistlessly appeal'd
　　To my young vivid fancy. 'Tis my doom—
A mournful one ! towards loveliness to hie,
Like a moth towards a candle—burnt thereby.

XIV.

She did indeed look lovely—yet away
　　I turned from her, and with her sire convers'd,
Until we Blackey's summons did obey
　　To dinner, which my gloom somewhat dispers'd ;
Our meal was like that of the previous day,
　　Of which the details need not be rehears'd—
The Major ate and grumbled, I ate too
In silence—Bill had something else to do.

XV.

He seem'd to feed on Bella's blushing face
　　Which was indeed a morsel all delicious—
Sadness I could in her behaviour trace,
　　For the necessity most unpropitious
Of his departure—tho' her usual grace
　　(For in her temper she was not capricious),
Flung o'er her every motion, an attraction
Which must have giv'n her lover satisfaction.

XVI.

I sat, like Lucifer at Eden's gate,
　　Gazing upon the Paradise within—
A witness of another's happy fate
　　Who'd won an Eve I would have died to win.
Alas ! that here I should have come thus late,
　　Was my reflection—now to love is sin—
And then with Bella I partook of wine,
To catch her glance, which beam'd on me, divine.

XVII.

And so we took our meal and then desert.
　　The ladies left us—talked our host and laugh'd ;
And, e'er to tell his deeds in war alert,
　　He boasted of his valour while he quaff'd
Glass after glass ; but us could not divert
　　From our reflections—" You must both be daft,"
At length he cried, " you neither speak a word ;
Cheer up ! this gloomy silence is absurd."

XVIII.

But still we silent sat till called to tea,
　　Which over, it was time to take the road—
Anxious from Bella's influence to flee,
　　No longer in the drawing-room I abode,
But to the yard betook myself to see
　　If were prepared the buggy for its load ;
I found old Adam harnessing our steed,
Again grown taciturn, and him I fee'd.

XIX.

When I re-entered, Bill was taking leave,
　　Which was, indeed, a mournful operation ;
And I saw Bella's graceful bosom heave
　　As they apart held whisper'd conversation.
Parting's a sad affair, and lovers grieve,
　　Thinking their hearts will break at separation :
I dar'd not look much at them, for already
Nervous I felt, to my resolve unsteady.

XX.

So to my host I turn'd, him bade farewell—
   Firmly he grasped my hand ; we separated ;
To my lot then his comely lady fell,
   Who said the pleasure she anticipated
Of my society again, to dwell
   In their vicinity, if I were fated.
And lastly Bella I approached—" Adieu !"
I cried, as to my lips her hand I drew.

XXI.

Bill saw us not, for he was in the hall.
   The buggy's wheels were sounding on the gravel.
I slipp'd out after him, as he did call
   To Bella, for it was my wish to travel.
A glimpse I caught, when outside, of her shawl,
   The fringe of which from Bill's coat to unravel
She seem'd.   Disconsolate I took my seat,
And out Bill sprang, his happiness complete.

XXII.

He took the reins from Adam, and beside me
   Was seated soon ; and so we left the door—
And to arrange my person I applied me.
   To ope the gate old Adam ran before.
Bill's smiling face seem'd almost to deride me,
   While to the high-road forth we sped once more ;
He crack'd his whip, and, o'er the level planking
We gaily bowl'd—the pace indeed was spanking.

XXIII.

The night was cloudy, so we had no moon
   To light us, as we homeward took our way ;
Upon the boards this matter'd not, but soon
   Our road along the lane uneven lay.
Here we went slowly, for the light of noon
   We'd prov'd might on its ruggedness betray—
It was a tiresome process, in the dark,
Where we might safely travel, well to mark.

XXIV.

We walk'd, however, and our horse Bill guided,
    So that we manag'd safely our progression ;
I have our lamps lighted as we had provided
    Before we started, danger of transgression
From the right track was less, as they supply did
    A flickering light to shine on our procession.
The cedar swamp, which daylight could not gladden
Gloomy enough looked then a sprite to sadden.

XXV.

And when, at length, we issued from the lane,
    Along the even road we gaily trotted
Until we reach'd the Humber. To remain
    A short time with mine host, as we had plotted
Before we started, and a glass to drain
    There—and, with rain too as it slightly spotted.
We check'd our hackney at the tavern door,
A shelter taking till the show'r was o'er.

XXVI.

We drank some grog, and stay'd about an hour,
    But fast and faster did the rain descend ;
'Twas useless waiting, for it was no show'r,
    But rain whose torrents *might* with morning end
A wet night had set in, the clouds did low'r,
    And darkness round th' horizon did extend ;
Therefore we thought 'twas best to brave the weather,
And in the buggy took our seats together.

XXVII.

Impatient was our steed to reach his stable,
    So his impetuosity to curb
Bill held the reins tightly as he was able,
    Fearing a " bolt" our journey should disturb,
Which the rain made for us uncomfortable
    Enough without that—till in the suburb
We were, which we had quitted of Toronto,
When, in high glee, the Humber we had gone to

XXVIII.

It chanc'd unluckily for us the street
    Had just been trench'd to lay a gas-pipe down ;
So a rough barrier progress did defeat,
    Into the gulph that those might not be thrown
Whom travelling, darkness to believe might cheat
    That all was level ; and to make this known
A lanthorn had afforded feeble light,
Which ere we drove up was extinguish'd quite.

XXIX.

Full on the fence we charg'd, before we knew
    Of its existence ; and the sudden shock
Me to the bottom of the gully threw
    Upon my feet. A single bruise or knock
I was not injur'd by—altho', 'tis true,
    My sudden fall (or I had been a block)
Rather astonish'd me, and made me doubt
A moment what on earth I was about.

XXX.

Experienc'd Bill, a more disastrous fate.
    The reins he held prevented from descending
His body—so he fell with all his weight
    Upon a post which tow'rds the street was bending.
His nose, unlucky feature, strange to state,
    In contact with the timber there extending
Came ; 'twas no wonder that the fall unnerv'd him
His face was bloody when I next observ'd him.

XXXI.

I need not say the vehicle was shattered.
    The horse had in the darkness disappear'd.
I only was excessively bespatter'd
    With mud—but that my friend was hurt I fear'd.
When I'd somewhat regain'd my senses scatter'd,
    Him I supported to a lamp that cheer'd
Th' obscurity around. There chanc'd to be
A tavern near, which I was glad to see.

XXXII.

We enter'd—Bill, of course, in piteous plight—
  He ask'd for water, which was quickly brought;
His visage was indeed a ghastly sight—
  'Twas well for him that Bella had not caught
Her first glimpse of him then, for with affright
  She'd fled the man who her affection sought.
Of blood he'd greatly suffer'd from the loss—his
Nose too was swoll'n to a huge proboscis.

XXXIII.

He bath'd his face till he had wash'd away
  The blood, which there had form'd a kind of crust ;
His features, thus discover'd, did display,
  Where on the post they had been lately thrust
A bruise discoloured ; as if, in a fray,
  After a beating, he had manag'd just
To save himself, not having gained much glory,
But in its stead a visage swoll'n and gory.

XXXIV.

He took a glass of brandy, neat, for faint
  The loss of blood and bruise had made him feel—
Then wished me to set forward, to acquaint
  Our host with what had happen'd—to reveal
The state his buggy then was in—to paint
  His own condition—(he could only reel
When he essay'd to walk)—he then would sleep,
For just up stairs, he thought, he p'rhaps might creep.

XXXV.

I went to Stone's—the landlord was irate,
  But soon perceiv'd that we were not to blame—
I said the buggy we'd reintegrate,
  Paying whate'er for damage he might claim.
Bill's horse was there before me, at the gate,
  Trembling with fear—he seem'd a little lame ;
Part of the buggy at his heels was hanging,
Which him had frightened, on the pebbles banging.

XXXVI.

Him we examin'd—nought but a slight bruise
　　Upon his heel he'd by th' upset receiv'd,
The hostler said he would some ointment use,
　　Which wounds of that sort always had relieved.
He led the animal on towards the mews,
　　And much o'er Bill's sad accident he griev'd—
To Mrs. Coulson I a message sent,
T' inquire with Harriet's ankle how it went.

XXXVII.

She sent her compliments—"Would I ascend,
　　And that her ankle was improving learn
From Harriet's lips?"—I answered I'd a friend
　　Whose state precarious gave me then concern,
Whom I must visit; but she might depend
　　On seeing me, when morning should return.
To Harriet kind wishes I dispatch'd,
And to see Bill from bliss myself I snatch'd.

XXXVIII.

In bed I found him; he was in great pain,
　　But wish'd to seek repose—I said, "good-night,"
And promis'd on the morrow him again
　　To see, and homeward went to take a slight
Repast ere I my own couch did attain.
　　Upon my way I saw a twinkling light,
Which I approach'd, and found the hostler there,
The buggy gazing at with rueful air.

XXXIX.

"It must stay here till morning," looking up,
　　Observ'd the functionary with a sigh;
"Yes," answer'd I—"but let us home to sup,
　　For bed-time, as you know, is drawing nigh;
I dare say at the bar you'll take a cup
　　At my expense." "Thanks, sir," was his reply—
And so tow'rds the hotel our way we wended,
Muttering the man, "It must be promptly mended."

XL.

I supp'd alone, thinking of her then near me—
    Should I, or should I not, my love declare ?
I drank a glass of whi-key-punch to cheer me,
    And long I sat in meditation there
Perplex'd. I took a pipe. Which way to steer me,
    I knew not, therefore, smok'd on the affair.
The wreath's of smoke now pictur'd Harriet's features —
Now Bella's—both, indeed, were lovely creatures.

XLI.

Now Harriet's fainting form and languid eye—
    Languid ! but oh, how lovely ! fill'd my soul.
Then Bella, fairy-like, was hovering nigh—
    Alas ! *not* mine—I could not all control
The fiend-like thought—Bill might be doom'd to die—
    Had from our Buggy we but chanc'd to roll
With so great force, that death had seiz'd on him,
How I'd have welcom'd e'n a fractur'd limb.

XLII.

" This will not do," said I, and fill'd my glass,
    " Bella, thy blue eyes shall be nought to me—
Like a sweet dream they from my mind *shall* pass,
    And now it *must* be morning. I'll be free—
Harriet, canst thou enslave me ? Yes, sweet lass,
    My heart grown constant shall return to thee—
I'll woo thee—win thee—ah ! the thought's divine,
Harriet, all doubt is fled, thou *shalt* be mine."

XLIII.

Such was my mood when I retir'd to rest—
    I soon was buried in a sleep profound ;
Nor woke until the sunbeams did attest
    Morning was gladd'ning every thing around.
I sprung from bed refresh'd, and quickly drest.
    Then down to breakfast eagerly did bound,
No longer doubting—but with mind at ease —
To what I'd purposed firm as fate's decrees.

XLIV.

When I had breakfasted I call'd on Bill,
　"Knight of the woful countenance," indeed,
He was—and felt himself extremely ill—
　To find a surgeon I did then proceed.
Whom I sent to him; then I loung'd until
　'Twas time to call on Harriet, as agreed.
With what alacrity the stairs I scaled;
With tap how gentle, too, the door assail'd!

XLV.

"Come in!"—the sound was music to my ear!
　"Come in!"—'twas melody itself she spoke!
"Come in!"—dispell'd was every doubt and fear!
　"Come in!"—my heart at once assum'd its yoke!
"Come in!"—what angel voice was whisp'ring near!
　"Come in!"—from fairy lips the accents broke!
"Come in!"—I enter'd, could I disobey
That charming mandate driving gloom away?

XLVI.

She was alone.　Her cheek was pale, which made
　Her large and lustrous eyes more lovely seem.
Her hair, upon her marble brow display'd,
　Her white hand propp'd; and you might almost deem,
Thro' those transparent fingers, that the shade
　Of the bands silken did obscurely gleam.
She was reclining when I came.　A start
Shew'd I was not unwelcome to her heart.

XLVII.

She blush'd, and started.　Her dilated eye
　Shone with a hue no words of mine can paint;
That eye, which varied so, it would defy
　The limner's art of it to give a faint
Conception, then all language did supply—
　She had no need of utterance to acquaint
Me with her feelings;—that she'd been neglected,
She thought I, in that glance of her's, detected.

XLVIII.

I strode across the room, and took her hand.

"Miss Coulson, you may think I've tarried long,"
I said, "but I will make you understand
    No fault it was of mine.   To stay, a strong
Objection I express'd, and even plann'd
    Duncan to leave his country friends among;
Returning here to make enquiry strict
About the sprain I aided to inflict.

XLIX.

" Your pale cheeks tell me you are yet unwel..
    A clumsy fellow I have been indeed,
T' have caus'd you here so long in pain to dwell;
    I really know not what excuse to plead—
An Angel was before me, and I fell,
    Of judgment with e'en less than Balaam's steed :
Will you accord me pardon?   Set at rest
My guilty conscience, and I shall be blest."

L.

Sweet was the smile she gave me.   " Pardon, yes!
    I think indeed I was as bad as you.
We both were very careless, I confess,"
    She answer'd, "such a foolish thing to do.
But let it pass ; do not, I pray, lay stress
    Upon so slight a sprain—quite well now, too,
Sir, I can walk most nimbly—almost dance—
P'rhaps after all it was a lucky chance.

LI.

" We know each other now   Our introduction
    Was of the strangest—but we must be friends.
An Angel! truly I'm an odd production
    For such.   An Angel from on high *descends*.
In your theology you need instruction,
    Which towards Idolatry too plainly tends.
I was a *Saint ascending*, when you met me,
Man, was it, sir, or Angel who upset me?"

LII.

"Man, certainly—at least his feelings now
    Are human all. He bends in adoration
(And here, to that sweet girl I made a bow,
    My eyes expressive of my admiration)
To the divinity on that fair brow
    Enshrin'd." She blushed, and turn'd the conversation.
We sat and chatted gaily till arriv'd
Her mother; and I thought my wooing thriv'd.

LIII.

To stay and dine with them I was invited.
    I did so; and the evening slipp'd away.
I left them, charm'd with Harriet, and delighted,
    And hasted to the house where Duncan lay.
He listen'd eagerly while I recited
    By his bedside my actions thro' the day.
To Bella he'd contriv'd to pen a letter,
Our fall describing, saying he was better.

LIV.

From him I went home to my lonely bed,
    Thinking of Harriet—really now in love,
All doubt, for ever, from my heart had fled.
    "My firm affection," said I, "time will prove,"
As on the pillow I repos'd my head;
    "She has had pow'r this craving heart to move.
I'll woo her—win her—let but fortune smile,
And——then sweet sleep my senses did beguile.

LV.

Day after day with that sweet girl I spent.
    The more I saw of her, the more my heart
Confess'd the flood of passion closely pent
    Within its core, which to me did impart
A sombre mood, again had found a vent.
    I linger'd near her, loathing to depart.
With her I walk'd. On horseback by her side
I rode. How swiftly did those glad days glide.

LVI.

We never spoke of love; but some excuse
    We found to be together. The same book
We read.   In mental gifts had been profuse
    Nature to Harriet; and in her look
Beam'd intellect.   To walk she would induce
    Me, with a volume, to some shelter'd nook,
And then would listen while I read to her,
Chain'd to the spot, without a wish to stir.

LVII.

Her soft, white hand would rest upon my arm,
    And her eyes gaze intently on my face.
Upon my cheek I felt her breathing warm;
    And when I ceas'd, she thank'd me with sweet grace
Oh! I could read for ages, with the charm
    Of such companionship—all lore could trace—
Nor heavy find my eyes, did Harriet sit
Beside me at my study, sweet'ning it.

LVIII.

Her mother saw all this—but we were young,
    So very young (I was not then *nineteen*,
Scarce sixteen Harriet), so she fondly clung
    To the delusion—oft in this world seen,
Or Bards have falsely their love-ditties sung—
    That nought of passion could arise between
A laughing girl—tho' pensive she became—
And a wild boy.   How purblind was the dame?

LIX.

She little knew, all boy as I appear'd,
    A widow'd heart was aching in my breast,
When her sweet daughter with her beauty cheer'd
    The desert spot, that I could yet be blest
Giving assurance—or she might have fear'd
    That roving boy, at times with gloom opprest;
Then gaily smiling, as if life were gladness,
Might make her daughter love him e'en to madness.

LX.

My own impression is, she never thought
    About the matter, till it was too late.
By chance to know each other we'd been brought,
    And on my character to speculate—
If such a mental process she'd been taught—
    Never once struck her; so it was our fate,
Mine and her daughter's, while she thought us friends,
Whither to shew such friendship surely tends.

LXI.

Thus pass'd a month. Bill was recover'd quite,
    And much he rallied me on the affair.
We saw each other seldom; for delight
    It was to me to Harriet to repair
Each morning, and I stay'd all day; and night
    Surprised me at her side still ling'ring there.
August insensibly away had glided,
When on a tour to go we all decided.

LXII.

Bright was the morning—gladly shone the sun ;
    The lake lay calmly sleeping, waveless, blue ;
The porters on the wharf did blithely run,
    As towards the steamboat our conveyance drew.
That day to me was a most joyous one,
    For I had nought but pleasure to pursue.
I must indeed have been a very churl,
To have felt sombre with that lovely girl.

LXIII.

The carriage stops. The driver from his seat
    Descends, and opens hastily the door ;
The lower'd steps receive my nimble feet ;
    I touch the wharf, and she whom I adore
Places her hand in mine—her ankle neat,
    Well from the sprain, and supple as before,
Is se t as from the vehicle she springs—
Her mother following to my shoulder clings.

LXIV.

The porters seize upon a trunk a-piece,
    Desirous each to ease us of his fee ;
Nor do these gentry from their labours cease,
    Until our luggage safe on board we see.
We pay them and the driver, and release
    The latter from attendance ; then on me
The ladies lean, the steamer's deck we gain,
And gaze delighted on the watery plain.

LXV.

The steam is up, and sounds the starting bell ;
    The ropes are loosen'd, and she cuts her way
Thro' the clear, placid waters, which to swell
    She causes as she glides into the bay.
She is a gallant boat, and swims full well,
    And briskly whirl the paddles in their play.
We reach the narrow strait—the main lake find—
Toronto and its bay are left behind.

LXVI.

Thy lake, Ontario's, a goodly sheet
    Of water—fresh, but like a sea expanding ;
Where hostile navies might manœuv'ring meet,
    Or ship's crews perish without chance of landing.
How lovely is thy smile ! but I have beat
    About thy waves, fearful my bark of stranding.
Those, who on voyage bent, have left the sea-shore,
Know, in a gale, what danger's in a lea-shore.

LXVII.

Long days and nights upon thy bosom toss'd
    My boat has labour'd—fled was every hope—
Those who my coming look'd for, thought me lost—
    Indeed 'twas fearful with that storm to cope.
Again thy sleeping wavelets I have cross'd,
    As then I did with Harriet, giving scope
To my "imagination's' airy play,"
As I went smoothly on my watery way.

LXVIII.

Our voyage was delicious. The warm sun
　　Shone with full power on the azure lake;
The breeze was fair, aiding the steamboat's run,
　　And cooling to us; so that it did make
The seat we occupied a pleasant one
　　Beneath the awning; and when Harriet spake,
The joyous smile her gladden'd bosom taught her,
Was like the rippling of that placid water.

LXIX.

We sat and gaz'd upon the distant shore,
　　Where the green woods were dipping in the wave—
I told her every feeling which came o'er
　　My heart—I was become that sweet girl's slave.
Oh! what romantic *nothings* did I pour
　　Into her ear, which close attention gave
To the fond boy, whose very life or death
Hung on that fairy creature's lightest breath.

LXX.

A jutting neck of land—a narrow strait—
　　We near'd, and soon were in a landlock'd bay.
We steam'd up this, nor did our speed abate
　　Till alongside the landing-place we lay.
Here carriages our coming did await,
　　To carry us to Hamilton away.
Short was the drive, and pleasant, to the town,
Where at a fine hotel we were set down.

LXXI.

It is a growing, thriving, busy place,*
　　With a rich country lying all around,
Is Hamilton; and in each eager face
　　An air of Yankee "smartness" may be found,
And in the stores a visitor may trace
　　Comfort and wealth the merchants do surround.
The streets are wide—the environs are pretty—
The whole is striking of this infant city.

* This description of Hamilton applies to it in 1845, when the Author visited
it—and all that part of Upper Canada.

LXXII

We stroll'd a' out the town, when we had taken
    Luncheon, observing all things to be seen,
Myself and Harriet (for too much shaken
    Was Mrs. C. to walk with us).   The green
And wooded hills, which on the horizon break in,
    Serve as a dark frame to the urban scene.
The market teemed with fruits and fragrant flowers—
A pleasant promenade that day was ours.

LXXIII.

When we had dined in private, and the wine
    Was plac'd before us, sparkling, luscious, glad—
Inspiring bright thoughts with its tide divine,
    Forbidding those who drank it to be sad,
Together we took counsel.   " Daughter, mine,"
    Said Mrs. Coulson, " is the highway bad
To London ?   You don't know! then pray enquire,
For to go there I feel a great desire.

LXXIV.

" As Mr. Turnbull is become our beau,
    I have been planning a delightful trip—
From Hamilton to London we will go ;
    Then to Port Stanley, where ourselves we'll ship
On board the boat which plies to Buffalo
    Whence——I declare you have contrived to sip
The wine from Mr. Turnbull's glass.   My dear
To what I'm saying to you, lend an ear !"

LXXV.

" Really, mamma, I have, I do declare—
    Oh ! yes, I'm listening," Harriet replied—
" The Falls, I think you said, we'd visit, where
    To be, for months past, I've in secret sigh'd ;
I'm sure, mamma, you said so—do not stare—
    Did she not say the Falls ?"   " No, no !" I cried.
" Well," said the blushing girl, "I have been dreaming,
And with the Falls my fancy has been teaming.

LXXVI.

" *The Falls* I was, indeed, about to name—
    Your dream somewhat prophetic seems, my love,"
Answer'd mamma—" our thoughts appear the same
    About the matter, so we'll go, I move—
And your assistance, sir, we ladies claim;
    (Turning to me) so your politeness prove,
By making on the morrow such enquiries
As may be requisite. This our desire is."

LXXVII.

" Agreed," I answer'd, " ere I go to bed
    I will descend the stairs, and, at the bar,
Will gain the knowledge you require. No dread
    Have that I'll fail you—trust to my cigar—
This evening it will on the subject shed
    Much light. Like Harriet, having come thus far,
To see Niagara I pant—I burn.
The Falls unvisited I'll not return."

LXXVIII.

The evening pass'd so rapidly, I started
    When the clock struck eleven.—" Come, my dear,
We must to bed, said Mrs. C." Departed
    The ladies. Then my solitude to cheer,
Down to the bar I stepp'd, jocund, light-hearted.
    Of course the bar-keeper was hovering near—
He mix'd my grog—a pure Havannah handed,
Then gave the information I demanded.

LXXIX.

The following evening there would be a stage
    (Coaches in Canada are called always
Stages) for London, in which to engage
    Places we should be able—for most days
Room there was ample in the equipage.
    The roads, he said, were good—beyond all praise,
Being stone and plank. It was a pleasant drive—
By noon the second day we should arrive.

P

LXXX.

" That will not suit," said I; " can we not go
  By day ?   The ladies may have an objection
By night to travel."   His reply was " No !
  The evening stage that runs in the direction
You wish to take carries the mails; and so
  The starting-time is not at the election
Of those who own it—'tis the sole conveyance
In which tow'rds London you can take your way hence."

LXXXI.

" If it be so, we must be satisfied,"
  I answer'd—as I hurried off to bed—
Not liking much the thought of a night's ride
  O'er *good* Canadian roads.   I'd had a dread
Of all-night trav'lling, since when I espied
  Bill's bloody face, and for assistance led
Him fainting from the Buggy.—That upset,
Was dwelling freshly in my memory yet.

LXXXII.

I told the ladies in the morning how
  The case stood with us—would they go or stay ? —
" Oh ! go, most certainly," cried Harriet, " now
  We are already so far on the way."
" What says Mamma," ask'd I—whose low'ring brow
  Misgivings of the project did betray—
" I do not like the journey," was her answer,
" But it must be, as we've no better plan, sir."

LXXXIII.

The day we pass'd as we'd spent the preceding,
  We walk'd and jok'd and chatted thro' the morning—
Then took our luncheon and a spell at reading—
  At least *I* did, for Harriet was adorning
With Berlin-work in wool a vest, —exceeding
  In beauty all I've seen, till time gave warning
That dinner was preparing—when she left me.
Of what a magic charm her going bereft me.

LXXXIV.

She left me, and I sat not long alone—
　　I hurried to my sleeping-room to make
Some change in my apparel, and I own
　　My looking-glass I did not there forsake
Till its reflection of my face had grown
　　Handsome enough a lady's heart to break.
" The vain young puppy !" some will here exclaim—
With reason—I confess it to my shame.

LXXXV.

We din'd, and presently the stage arriv'd ;
　　And a great clumsy vehicle it prov'd,
To stow ourselves within it we contriv'd,
　　And lumb'ring o'er the street away it mov'd.
We were its only inmates, and derived
　　From this some consolation.　My belov'd
Slept calmly soon ; and the bright moonbeams play'd
On the still features of the tranquil maid.

LXXXVI.

Would that I were a moonbeam, was the thought
　　That struck me, as the silvery gleams illum'd
Her parted lips, which the effulgence caught,
　　And a sweet, dreamy, amorous smile assum'd.
That cold cold beam may kiss the lips which ought
　　On me alone to shed their breath perfum'd—
That light may ravish the fair peach-like cheek,
An Eden my lips *would*, but *dare not* seek !

LXXXVII.

Hours there I sat entranc'd—gazing on her
　　Unconscious of the beauty she display'd ;
In truth I was spell-bound, and dare not stir
　　To break her slumber so profound, afraid.
Gently she woke at last—and I aver
　　No lovelier scene e'er broke, than we survey'd,
On mortal ken.　The moon, declining, rested
On the tall forest which dark foliage crested.

LXXXVIII.

A valley was around us—and a river
  Thro' it, impetuous, roll'd its murm'ring tide
Of limpid water, in whose waves did quiver
  The faint moonbeams, playing before they died.
A pause! The light grew fainter; for the giver
  Of those erratic gleams the forest wide
In its dark bosom had received, and gloom
O'ershadow'd all, and did the scene entomb.

LXXXIX.

"How lovely!" broke from Harriet's lips. "Indeed
  It was most lovely," said I, and dispos'd
My limbs to rest, of which I had great need.
  "Good night," I cried; and then my eyes I clos'd.
"Good night," she answer'd—so we both agreed
  Slumber to court; and on our seats repos'd.
The glad sun shining brightly through the boughs
Of the tall trees did me from sleep arouse.

XC.

Soon I saw clearings, then a house or two,
  Then a wide plain dotted with stumps of trees—
I nudg'd my fair companion's elbow, who
  Was slumb'ring still. "See," said I to her, "these
Extensive clearings we are driving thro',
  Prove (she awoke had with a yawn and sneeze)
We are about to reach our destination."
"Yes! this is London," was her exclamation.

XCI.

Houses of framework—a long, dirty street
  Appear'd—and down the latter to its end
We drove, when turning, the hotel did greet
  Us. Its façade some distance did extend.
We stopp'd—I quitted hastily my seat,
  Opening the door that we might all descend.
I sprang upon the *trottoir*—plank, of course,
Just as the hostler reach'd the near fore-horse.

XCII.

I handed out the ladies—paid the driver—
    We enter'd the hotel, and wrote our names
In a large book, plac'd that each new arriver
    Might add *his* autograph, or *her's* if 'twere a dame's.
Th' hotel was built of wood; and its contriver,
    The planks had ill-adapted to the frames,
So that the staircase shook as we ascended,
And a break-down I almost apprehended.

XCIII.

We reach'd our chambers safely—my toilette
    Arrang'd, I soon at Harriet's side was seated.
We took an early dinner, and then set
    Out to explore, leaving mamma, who heated
And tired with her journey could not yet
    Walk with us; so to her bed-room retreated.
Thro' a small square we went, then gain'd a road,
Down which we pass'd to where the river flow'd.

XCIV.

The Thames! the silv'ry Thames! a gentle stream,
    Unlike its world-known namesake in our isle,
Shallow and placid, a contrast extreme,
    To Britain's famous river! With a smile
I gaz'd upon the brook—my wildest dream
    Of insignificance surpass'd, the while,—
I'd heard this Western Thames described; yet vision
Made me regard it with intense derision.

XCV.

" Is this your Thames?" said I to Harriet. " This?—
    What could its sponsors think of when they nam'd
This pretty brook—which travellers might miss.
    ' The Thames!' The Thames! I really am asham'd
Of your Canadian river." " Yet it is
    A stream of too much beauty to be blam'd,"
She answer'd quickly, " for a vile misnomer,
That makes it a byeword to every roamer."

XCVI.

I thought of London Bridge—the pool below,
   The docks where ships repair from ev'ry shore.
The busy wharves—the steamers to and fro
   Gliding, at intervals, the water o'er.
And then I gaz'd where placidly did flow
   That gentle stream which never vessel bore—
I could have forded it, nor damp'd my knee,
" What's in a name," I said, "you here may see."

XCVII.

We turn'd our footsteps tow'rds the town again,
   Thro' which we went. I notic'd then but three
Brick houses*—London built upon a plain,
   Where lately was not fell'd a single tree ;
No mansions but of wood did then contain,
   Save the brick trio. Thus from the *debris*
Of the majestic woods—by man laid low,
Man had compell'd a thriving town to grow.

XCVIII.

We found mamma awaiting our return—
   She had been sleeping, and recover'd quite
From her fatigue, presided at the urn—
   A pleasant tea we took ; and then till night
We arrang'd all things for our short sojourn
   At London, looking forward with delight,
To thy cascade, Niag'ra, to afford us
Pleasure which should for all our toil reward us.

XCIX.

The following day was spent in London. Then
   The second morning, in a stage, we started
To gain Port Stanley—smiled all Nature when
   On our tour onward briskly we departed.
By the road-side the clearings met our ken,
   From which the harvest had been lately carted ;
The verdant foliage glisten'd in the sun,
The day indeed was a most glorious one!

---

* This was in 1843.

C.

The steamboat, at Port Stanley, alongside
　　The quay our stage's coming was awaiting—
So that at once on board of her we hied
　　While with our luggage were the porters freighting
Her cabin—"Let us choose our berths," I cried,
　　Amid the din the sailors were creating—
Then we the stairs descended, and inspected
The sleeping quarter's, and our own selected.

CI.

The steam is up—the vessel cuts the wave,
　　The azure waters of Lake Erie flash
In the bright sun, as they our steamer lave
　　Made tremulous as she does thro' them dash—
The wheels are whirl'd round briskly as they brave
　　The mimic billows with assiduous splash—
The bold white cliffs in distance are receding
As we swift on our voyage are proceeding.

CII.

'Tis noon—we dine—and when the meal is over—
　　We gain the deck and gaze on the still lake—
Evening comes on and finds us at Port Dover,
　　Where we on board some passengers do take—
Beneath the moon and stars to be a rover,
　　While the white cresting foam defines your wake,
And the soft summer-breeze just moves the air
Upon that water, with a lady fair

CIII.

As a companion, who, confiding, clings
　　To your arm for support; whose gentle voice
Strikes on the ear melodious, while it brings
　　A feeling to the heart which says—"rejoice,"
Sublime indeed is—touching the deep springs
　　Of glad sensation.—Oh! had I my choice
Between such joy, and worldly wealth or fame—
The former, with what ardour would I claim.

CIV.

But it is night, and we must seek repose—
    I gain'd my berth, and into slumber sank,
No dream disturb'd me after I did close
    My eyelids—all till morning was a blank—
And when, refresh'd and jocund, I arose,
    By my bedside I paus'd, kind Heaven to thank
For all the blessings which on me did flow,
Then gain'd the deck as we near'd Buffalo.

CV.

The mists were curling upward from that sheet
    Of sleeping water, and the morning sun
Was looming hazily my eyes to greet
    Thro' the thin shroud of vapour, which begun
To melt before it—that my gaze did meet,
    Was the lake's aspect, a heart-gladd'ning one.
As toward the port we steer'd, sloop, brig, and steamer,
Flung on the gentle breeze full many a streamer.

CVI.

'Twas Sunday morning, yet when we arrived,
    The wharves were crowded with a busy throng.
No Sabbatarians there would have contriv'd
    To make men dearly pay for doing wrong.
Sir Andrew Agnew ne'er would have surviv'd
    The traffic had he seen, which we along
The streets observ'd—"shops open" was the fashion.
For Sunday-trading there appeared a passion.

CVII.

We did not tarry long at the hotel,
    To which by omnibus we were convey'd,
But just took dinner, and ere evening fell,
    Thro' the main streets myself and Harriet stray'd.
Summoned to church we were by many a bell
    But went not, for my love was sore afraid
Of venturing amid strangers—she was shy,
So to Mamma at the hotel would hie.

CVIII.

We pass'd the night there, look'd about next day,
    But saw not much t' attract in Buffalo.
Nought was there to invite a lengthen'd stay.
    We had no business, so prepar'd to go
After we'd din'd; and took again our way
    Down to the wharf; and soon our trunks did stow
On board the steamboat, with the aid of porters—
Then chose ourselves on deck commodious quarters.

CIX.

The steamer plied to Schlosser; a place noted
    In history now—for there the " Caroline "
Lay during the rebellion; and devoted
    Was to destruction. Other pens than mine
This incident at large have long since quoted,
    So on it I'll not spend another line.
The afternoon was lovely, and invited
Our gaze the shores on which we look'd delighted.

CX.

I pause. No human pen has ever limn'd,
    No human pencil has had pow'r to paint
The river o'er whose sparkling waves we skimm'd.
    Gladly I would depict it; give a faint
Resemblance of th' original, which dimm'd
    My eyes as they gaz'd on it—would acquaint
The reader with the grandeur of that stream
Which looms before me, a majestic dream.

CXI.

But words are all too feeble to essay
    Even a sketch of that which must be *seen*,
Unseen it cannot be conceived. Away
    With language!—Who has ever been
Where thy wild waters in delirium play,
    Niagara, the States, and Canada between,
Without confessing all description vain,
Of scenes whose outlines mind cannot retain.

CXII.

A river! 'Tis a chain of inland seas
    Into whose bosom countless rivers pour,
Their tribute! The collected volume these
    Dash thro' a narrow strait. The distant roar
Of the cascade is borne upon the breeze.
    A line of rapids borders either shore,
Foaming and sparkling in the summer sun.
This was their aspect on our downward run.

CXIII.

And Navy Island, cover'd with dense wood,
    With here and there a patch of shelving green,
Treeless, expanding tow'rds the mighty flood
    Which it divides, an island gem is seen.
We pass it—still more angry in its mood
    The torrent grows—short space does intervene
Of boiling rapids; then that wond'rous fall,
Unrivalled upon earth, engorges all.

CXIV.

We turn'd to Schlosser—at the rapid's head.
    'Tis but a landing-place—no building there
Is seen. Around dense coppices are spread.
    A stage conveys the tourists who repair
To the not distant village. So we sped
    On to that village, near the cascade, where,
At the hotel the carriage set us down,
Which owes its custom to the Falls renown.

CXV.

When we had gain'd the hotel and taken tea,
    'Twas evening, and the moon began to shine;
Plac'd at the open window—gazing, we,
    To the Falls roar our ears did all incline.
" Oh! 'twould be glorious," exclaimed I, " to see
    The cataract by moonlight." " The design
I will not count'nance," said Mamma, excited,
" For Harriet's safety I shall feel affrighted."

CXVI.

" Let us sit here to-night, or you can go
    (Turning to me), but Harriet must not stir—
If, in the morning, you will act the *beau*,
    You shall survey the cataracts with her;
For some time past I've yearly seen them, so
    That pleasure I can willingly defer,
The ferry till we cross—*yourself* to-night
May see them, if to do so give delight."

CXVII.

' Oh! no, I'll wait for Harriet," I replied,
    " The Falls are an attraction, it is true,
But," whisper'd I (as nearer to her side,
    To gain her ear, my chair I gently drew),
" There is a greater here." A blush to hide
    She rais'd her hand.—I'm confident she knew,
Words would be spoken by that thundering Fall,
Which neither boy nor girl could ere recall.

CXVIII.

We sat in silence, looking on the trees,
    Which there grew scatter'd in an open grove—
Just gently faun'd our cheeks the evening breeze.
    My soften'd heart was all attun'd to love—
That fair girl by my side, my fancy sees,
    As it discursive o'er the past does rove—
Her fairy form—her open marble brow,
And her sweet blushing cheek, as I write now.

CXIX.

1 went to bed, but found not there repose—
    The cataract was roaring in my ear—
Vainly I courted sleep—my lids to close
    Was easy—but—Niagara was near!—
Near but unseen. I do not envy those
    With such a wondrous scene their eyes to cheer
When they should rise, who could to slumber sink—
All I could do was on the morn to think.

CXX.

Night pass'd—the longest night *must* pass away.

As morning dawn'd a troubl'd sleep came o'er me,

Which bound my senses till it was full day.

Niagara, thy falls, appear'd before me.

As, dreaming on my tumbled couch I lay,

A cascade I created.   Fancy bore me

To an ideal scene, grand, sublime, exciting.

Harriet was with me my fond eye delighting.

CXXI.

A tapping at the door—" 'Tis eight o'clock,"

In a soft female voice destroy'd the vision.

I sprang from bed—repeated was the knock—

" I'm rising," in a tone of great decision,

Said I—the door proceeding to unlock.

As if struck by the wand of a magician,

The girl had vanish'd—ere what she had brought,

My shaving water, in my hand I'd caught.

CXXII.

To shave, to dress—to hurry down the stairs

Took me not long.   Already at the table

Mamma and Harriet were commencing theirs,

Attended there by an assistant sable,

Who, his teeth shining stood behind their chairs,

And seem'd to think all things were comfortable.

To both I gave the morning salutation,

To which responded they with animation.

CXXIII.

We took our meal in haste.   The sun was shining,

The weather was for our design propitious.

" Do, Harriet, go and dress," said I, repining

At the least loss of time.   " The day's delicious."

Off ran the merry girl—my thoughts divining.

" Mamma, a pleasant morning don't you wish us ?"

Cried I, as took my arm her lovely daughter—

Perfect in beauty, then, indeed I thought her.

CXXIV.

" Yes," was the answer, and th' hotel we quitted,
    And hurried on, impatient, to the Fall,
Fast as the ground o'er which we walk'd permitted.
    We gain'd the river's side ; and at our call
The Ferry-boat appear'd.   A station fitted
    We thought the mid-stream for a view of all.
A ladder we descended—reach'd the boat,
And soon below the cauldron were afloat.

CXXV.

When in the stream, at first—I am asham'd
    To tell my feelings—the cascades were not
What I had dream'd them.   But their grandeur claim'd,
    After a pause, such wonder as no spot
I've seen from me could wring.   Let not be blam'd
    Niagara for this.   It is no blot
On its surpassing majesty.   The mind
Must grow more ample far ere it can find

CXXVI.

Room to contain the vastness of the scene.
    The silvery mass of water which descends,
Goat Island, and the village shore, between,
    Like a huge curtain, whose full drapery blends
With pictur'd foam beneath, appears to lean
    Upon some hidden bar, from which it sends
Its watery folds to mingle with the stream,
Flashing and sparkling in the solar gleam.

CXXVII.

The little *Hog's Back* Fall—a line of light—
    Between its mighty neighbours meets the eye,
A thing to gaze on with intense delight—
    A pleasing contrast to the monsters nigh ;
But when the Horse-shoe Fall breaks on the sight
    In all its huge proportions, by and by,
Astonishment profound, with pleasure mixed,
You feel at that on which your eye is fixed.

CXXVIII.

And awe! For the huge mass of tumbling foam,
    Circling descends, magnificent, below.
And should the eye enquiring upwards roam,
    The mists of spray with varied rainbows glow ;
And to your mind when you the truth bring home,
    That down those rocks vast inland seas do flow.
The scene—the thoughts—o'erwhelm th' enraptur'd soul,
Which humbl'd feels near that stupendous whole.

CXXIX.

We sat and gaz'd. Then turn'd us to the shore,
    Whence we had come ;—which gain'd, the rocks we scal'd,
Pausing to take a farewell look before
    The view was hidden which had just assail'd
Our wondring eyes. A wooden bridge spans o'er
    Th' American cascade, and we avail'd
Ourselves of this, the centre isle to gain,
Where of both Falls we might a view obtain.

CXXX.

On Goat Island is built a paper-mill,
    Work'd by the stream that downward rushes there.
Where reigns the " Beautiful," the Yankees still
    In the pursuit of *dollars* take good care,
To bend the falling water to their will,
    So that for sale it something may prepare.
" The privilege " is doubtless one of worth ;
Indeed, I know no other such on earth.

CXXXI.

We crossed the Island and the shelving rock
    I stepped on, leaving Harriet to gain
The tower built amid the waters' shock,
    Whence of the Horse-Shoe Fall I did obtain
A glorious view. Below th' abyss did mock
    My vision's strength, tho' I my eyes did strain
To catch the cauldron hidd'n in foam and spray,
Till I grew dizzy, and so turn'd away.

CXXXII.

Above, the rapids the Canadian shore
 Line for some distance, and across the stream
Extend until their foam comes toppling o'er
 The precipice, one, as of which we dream.
I felt a wild delight ne'er felt before,
 As the spray struck me, and the flood did gleam
Beneath my feet—array'd in all its glory
I seem'd a river God of Grecian story.

CXXXIII.

From stone to stone I stepp'd—pausing awhile
 On each, to gaze above, around, below ;
And Harriet stood, impatient, on the side
 Looking upon me, and did fearful grow.
Caution she urg'd aloud.   A scornful smile
 Was my reply, as I did forward throw
My foot in act to spring.   I gain'd her side
When me for rashness she began to chide.

CXXXIV.

And she blush'd sweetly, as she ceas'd to speak.
 She had betray'd the feelings of her heart—
I read affection on her crimson'd cheek,
 And this did confidence to me impart.
" Words," said I, " sweetest love, are all too weak
 To speak my feelings.   Be assur'd thou art
Dearer to me than life, or wealth, or fame.
That hand of thine is all the prize I claim."

CXXXV.

She gave it, and I pressed it to my lips.
 I wound my arm around her, and I kiss'd
Her cheek, her brow.   How total the eclipse
 Was of the Falls to us !   Her slender wrist
I held—which felt delicious to the tips
 Of my enamour'd fingers.   " I insist
On one kiss more," I said.   Her mouth presented
My charmer.   What I did my heart contented.

THE END.